Dear Reader

As soon as I stayed there, and met newborn babies and beaming new fathers in the lift, I wanted to write a book set in the Baby Hotel.

It's not really called that, but it's real. It's a lovely four-star beachfront hotel that also keeps a few beds where mums can choose to transfer soon after having a baby. As it's a hotel and not a hospital this allows them to have their families stay with them while they settle in with their new baby. And Mum doesn't have to do the housework! There's a midwife available twenty-four hours a day for help, and of course the hotel provides food and housekeeping. I thought it was a lovely idea for those mums who don't want to rush home but miss their family too much to stay in hospital.

I also found it was a great place for heroes to hang out. Even royal princes!

My midwife, Carmen, meets Zafar, a gorgeous widowed sheikh from the land of Zandorro, at the Baby Hotel. He's arrived to bring his cousin back to their homeland to keep her safe, and decides that Carmen is the perfect person to return with them and help the new mum settle in with her twins.

This is my first Sheikh book, and I smiled all the way through—especially at Carmen's refusal to be over-awed by the prestige of Zafar, and Zafar's bafflement. There's baddies and goodies, and twins and births, and a little bit of luxury we can all dream about. I hope you enjoy your visit to the Baby Hotel and to the land of Zandorro as much as I did.

With warmest wishes

Fi xx

A mother to five sons, **Fiona McArthur** is an Australian midwife who loves to write. Mills & Boon® Medical™ Romance gives Fiona the scope to write about all the wonderful aspects of adventure, romance, medicine and midwifery that she feels so passionate about—as well as an excuse to travel! Now that her boys are older, Fiona and her husband, Ian, are off to meet new people, see new places, and have wonderful adventures. Fiona's website is at www.fionamcarthur.com

Also by Fiona McArthur:

SURVIVAL GUIDE TO DATING YOUR BOSS
HARRY ST CLAIR: ROGUE OR DOCTOR?
MIDWIFE, MOTHER...ITALIAN'S WIFE*
MIDWIFE IN THE FAMILY WAY*
THE MIDWIFE AND THE MILLIONAIRE
MIDWIFE IN A MILLION

Lyrebird Lake Maternity

**These books are also available in eBook format
from www.millsandboon.co.uk**

FALLING FOR THE SHEIKH SHE SHOULDN'T

BY
FIONA McARTHUR

First published in Great Britain 2012
by Mills & Boon, an imprint of Harlequin (UK) Limited.
Harlequin (UK) Limited, Eton House, 18-24 Paradise Road,
Richmond, Surrey TW9 1SR

© Fiona McArthur 2012

ISBN: 978 0 263 22692 8

Harlequin (UK) policy is to use papers that are natural, renewable and recyclable products and made from wood grown in sustainable forests. The logging and manufacturing process conform to the legal environmental regulations of the country of origin.

Printed and bound in Great Britain
by CPI Antony Rowe, Chippenham, Wiltshire

To Trishabella—who makes me smile.

CHAPTER ONE

THE lift doors opened. Prince Zafar Aasim Al Zamid stepped inside and to his disgust his heart began to pound.

Someone slipped past him into the elevator and he couldn't help the deeper breath he took as the doors shut. A drift of orange soap vividly recalled the memory of fruit-laden trees in the palace grounds as a child, and, by association, the memory soothed him.

Thoughts that calmed were an excellent idea. Life had been much less complicated then. He opened his eyes as the lift shifted under his feet.

Lately he'd been acquiring phobias like new shirts. Since the crash it had been heights, now elevators—worse every ascent—until even a closing door caused symptoms. Perhaps it was a sign the claustrophobia in his life had worsened since he'd been forced to give up his work in favour of royal duty.

He would address his inner calm with the solitude of a retreat as soon as he sorted this latest mess. The vastness of the desert always made his problems seem less significant.

For the moment he was cramped and palpitating in a lift with the painful reminder of all he'd lost. This particular enclosed space held a fragile-looking new mum with a baby in one arm, a beaming new father clutching a balloon, and thankfully the orange-scented woman as well, dispensing an aura of tranquillity.

The metallic 'It's A Boy' helium balloon bobbed towards him and Zafar leant closer to the wall and regretted his decision to stay at this hotel. A baby hotel. The last place he needed to be. The image he carried of his tiny son's body flickered in his mind and he forced it away. Such happy families were constant reminders he could have done without but the stakes were high.

He had hoped to find Fadia, his estranged cousin, prior to the birth but time was against him. He'd discovered she planned to convalesce here instead of hospital if he arrived too late to find her beforehand.

The lift jerked and his pulse thundered in his ears.

The balloon wielder tugged on the string as the proud new dad hailed the woman. 'Carmen! We didn't get a chance to thank you.' He grabbed the woman's hand and shook it vigorously. 'You were amazing.'

The woman retrieved her hand and smiled at the young mother. 'Hello, again, Lisa, Jock. Lisa was the amazing one.'

Her voice soothed like a cool hand to his forehead and, infinitesimally, a little more of his agitation drained away as the phobia receded. Thankfully. It would be useful if his psyche finally accepted the obscenity of irrational fears.

'It was a beautiful birth.' She cast Zafar a swift apologetic look for their exclusive conversation, and the unexpected impact of her one glance collided with his, as if that ridiculous balloon had bumped him, before she turned back to the father.

Medical background, he concluded, and dismissed the stab of frustration the loss of his career left him with. Midwife probably. He'd met women like her before—those natural soothers who could create a rapport with strangers without effort.

He lifted his head and glanced over her. Anything was good to take his mind off the ascent through the lift well.

Thankfully his phobia retreated by the second as he studied her. She had thick black hair coiled on her head like rope. An Irish accent. Carmen seemed more Spanish than Irish yet she suited her name.

He watched her mouth as she said, 'How is young Brody?'

Jock laughed, loudly, and Zafar winced as the noise jarred his ears. 'He's a bruiser.' The father's pride resonated within the four walls as the lift stopped at the fifth floor with an extra jolt. The cage floor fell six inches and bounced before it came back to the level. Everyone laughed nervously, except Zafar. He closed his eyes and swallowed.

There was rustling and movement as the lift emptied and the father's voice, a little further away now. 'We'll see you soon, then.'

'I'll be down as soon as I have handover report from the morning midwife.' So Carmen was still in the lift. He opened his eyes as she waved at the couple.

'That's great. We'll see you then.' Zafar noted the relief in the father's face and his mind clutched at the distraction of wondering about this trend of moving postnatal women from the hospital into hotels to recover from birth.

Not something he was familiar with but it made sense

when he thought about it. A place of quiet comfort, fewer germs, useful for the hospital to have quick turnover and quite appropriate if your health fund covered it.

The lift doors closed silently, though the cage remained stationary, and he returned to contemplate the lights on the panel above the door despite the insidious desire to study the woman called Carmen more closely.

She stepped back and seemed to lean into the wall.

He knew she was tall because her head came above his shoulders and her knot of hair had been near his nose as she'd drifted orange blossom his way. The lift still didn't move. Seconds to go and he would be able to breathe properly again.

He glanced at her from under his lashes and saw her eyes were shut. He frowned. Not a usual occurrence when he shared space with a woman. In fact, he couldn't remember the last time he'd been ignored. In repose she appeared weary. Too weary?

His concern increased. 'Are you unwell?'

Her eyes flew open and she straightened. 'Good grief.' She blinked at him and then focussed. 'A micro-sleep. Sorry. I've been on night shift. It's been a busy week.'

Suddenly he felt empathetic to a perfect stranger because he could remember that weariness from a string of busy days and nights during his internship. Lack of sleep he'd grumbled about, but now the choice was no longer his, he'd love to suffer from that inconvenience again.

That was the problem with returning to Sydney. It reminded him that he wasn't living the life he'd once loved. Made him feel frustration he shouldn't feel towards his duty to Zandorro.

The elevator jerked, ground upwards for a few inches. The sooner the better, he thought, then the lift bounced suddenly as the cable stopped.

His breath caught as he waited. The doors didn't open and the light sat on neither five nor six. Midway between floors. Stopped.

This was not good. He felt his heart rate shift gear, double before his next breath, his chest tightened, and air jammed in his lungs.

'I am so not in the mood for this.' Zafar heard her in the distance as he tried to loosen his throat. He sank down onto his haunches and put one hand on the wall to give himself more blood to his head. With his other he loosened his collar.

The lift was suddenly the cabin of the private jet. His family would plunge in a few spiralling seconds and there was not a thing he could do about it. So now it was his destiny to die. It was almost a relief. And he'd complained about being in line for the throne.

Distantly he realised she'd picked up the phone and spoken to the operator. When he heard her re-seat the instrument she bent down to him. 'You okay?'

He didn't refocus his eyes off the floor until he felt her hand on his arm—warm, firm, comfort personified—and not letting go. He had the bizarre idea he couldn't fall anywhere while she held him. Yet all she did was share touch without moving. He breathed with difficulty through his nose and inhaled drifts of orange. Incredibly steadying, like a shot of Valium through his bloodstream.

He sucked air through clenched teeth and the light-headedness faded a little. This was ridiculous. Irrational. Acutely embarrassing. He forced himself to look into her face. She had dark golden eyes, like burnt twisted treacle, calm and wise and filled with compassion. Mesmerising up close. 'You're a nurse?'

Her eyes crinkled and his chest eased a little more. 'Sort of. I'm a midwife. Do you need some deep breathing?'

'I'm not in labour.' But this was hard work. He shut his eyes again. 'Possibly.'

'Do you have a phobia?' The same gentle conversational voice as if she'd asked if he needed sugar in his tea.

The demons from the past battered against him. He strove to keep his voice level. 'So it seems.'

She sank down. He heard the rustle of fabric and felt the slight brush of her leg as she settled herself beside him on the floor. Her hand rested still on his arm, not moving, as if to transfer energy and calmness from her to him. It seemed to be working. 'What's your name?

He had many. 'Zafar.'

She paused and he felt her appraisal until he opened his eyes again. Her golden interest captured his. 'Well, Zafar. I'm Carmen. I've been stuck in this lift three times this week. Big, deep breaths should help.'

Deep breaths might be difficult. 'It is a battle with small ones.'

Coaxing. 'You can do a couple.'

He wasn't sure but the fact that she'd lived through this three times did help. He was feeling faint again. 'A rule of threes?'

'In through your nose...'

Intolerably bossy woman. 'Out through my mouth. Yes, I know.'

Her voice firmed. Like his mother's from the distant past. The time of orange trees. 'Then do it.'

He humoured her. And felt better. Actually, quite a lot better so he did it again. With her sitting below him he had a delightful view down the valley between her breasts. He glanced away politely but could feel himself improve every second with the picture in his mind. Surely a harmless medicinal remedy.

Imagine if the lift had still been full. He mentally shuddered. There was just her to see this weakness. Thankfully he'd sent his bodyguard and secretary to the suite. In future the stairs would be good for his fitness. Once free, he'd never see this woman again. A good thing, and a shame.

At least it seemed his brain had accepted death was unlikely.

And she had the most incredible breasts but he wasn't going to look again—his gaze travelled back to her face—and a delightful mouth. Those lips… His body stirred. A mouth designed by angels and plump for surrender if he was willing to risk life and limb for it. She may be calm but she looked very capable of protecting herself despite the weariness. His lips twitched.

'Are you feeling better?'

'Much.' Better than she knew. He watched with some amusement as she slowly recognised the direction of his fascination until she stared straight back at him and raised her brows.

She removed her hand from his arm and she shook her head. 'Tsk tsk.'

The lift jerked and resumed its ascent. Zafar shut his eyes briefly but the panic had gone.

It seemed she was good at her job. He straightened

until he stood with his feet firm beneath him, reached down and took her hand to help her up. Such a lovely hand, but workworn. She rose fluidly into his space, as he'd intended.

For that moment as their glances met he forgot the lift, the heights, the strain his life was, all except this unexpected awareness between them that swept away their surroundings, so enmeshed in this unexpected connection that when he said, 'Thank you,' the words hung in the air between them like mist.

An imp of mischief drew his head closer. He expected her to pull away. 'You're very kind…and incredibly beautiful.' He stroked her cheek, his gaze drawn once more to her ripe and luscious mouth.

She did the unpredicted. 'It's okay. I understand.' He heard it in her voice, a note of sympathy that horrified him. Pity?

He recoiled. He needed no one's compassion.

The elevator jolted and the doors opened on seven. They'd missed six altogether. She turned away from him with a frown on her entrancing face.

There was some consolation in the way she compressed her lips together as if to hide the way they'd plumped and reddened in anticipation…of what? The almost brush of his lips on hers? So she had felt something too?

'You certainly look better.' Her comment made him smile again, the dryness hiding undertones he couldn't identify, but there was a subtle flush of colour to her cheeks and her wide eyes searched his face as if seeking a hint of what had passed between them during the last few frozen moments.

Despite his urge to throw himself out of the lift to

safety, Zafar stretched his hand across the doors to allow her to precede him. 'My apologies for my weakness earlier.'

She assessed him with a clinical scrutiny he wasn't used to getting from a woman and strangled back a half-laugh. 'I doubt you're a weak man so I'm sure you've good reason.'

He inclined his head.

She glanced around. 'And I should have got out at level six.' She turned swiftly out to the left of the lift and pulled open the door of the fire escape to go down a flight before he was fully out of the lift himself.

He started to hum. The day was not as bad as it had started out.

Carmen moved quickly to reach the door to the stair-well but she could almost feel the eyes of the man in the lift on her back.

What had just happened? Her lips tingled as if still waiting and she could detect the unusual spicy after-shave from his skin so close to hers. And what a mouth! Sinful was too tame a word. She couldn't pretend she hadn't been tempted.

Not the sort of encounter she'd expected today and she wasn't entirely sure she'd behaved properly. Hopefully she wouldn't see him again.

When the fire-escape door shut with an echoing clang she breathed a sigh of relief as she leant back against it. Cold metal against her back was lovely to counter the heat everywhere else in her body. She glanced around.

Appropriate name. Fire escape.

She definitely felt a bit singed on the edges—like a

ragged sleeve too close to a candle—ragged and breath-less. She touched her lips. Burnt and hot without even touching him.

She glanced around again, reassured in a dark stair-well with unpainted concrete stairs and the echo of empty walls, but there was no doubt she was glad of the sanctuary afforded her.

One would have thought she'd learnt her lesson from her ex-husband about smooth-talking men in expensive suits who seduced you and then destroyed your life.

Still. One almost slip didn't make a disaster. She hoped.

Eighteen hours later Carmen O'Shannessy admired the gifts Mother Nature had bestowed on her at five that morning with a soft smile. She knew there was a rea-son she loved night duty, apart from the fact it allowed her to do two jobs.

Twins. Dark-haired cherubs with skin like dusky rosebuds. Her patient, Fadia Smith, rested back in the armchair like Madonna with her sons poking out under her arms like tiny bundled wings. It had taken a little juggling, a few attempts, and almost an hour of pa-tience, but with both boys feeding well this moment was a very satisfying end to a drama-filled morning.

It had been a long time since Carmen had seen twins born with so little fuss but, then, Fadia hadn't left them with much choice. Her cumbersome arrival alone and a bare five minutes before her first son appeared had left Carmen literally catching the baby. By the time the obstetrician and his entourage had arrived, number two had also decided to greet the outside world and Dr Bennett had waved her on with an incredulous smile.

To continue their no-fuss arrival, both wee boys had cried and then settled on their mother's skin. While they appeared small, there were no signs of prematurity or respiratory distress.

That would be unlike the breathless-from-running neonatal staff, who'd drifted back to their unit unneeded shortly afterwards. Carmen still smiled over their shock when she'd rung for help.

Two hours later Carmen should've been feeling ready to hand Fadia over to the day staff and go home. 'You sure I can't phone someone for you?' Something niggled.

Fadia seemed very sad. On cue with the question, Fadia jumped in the chair and the two babies stopped their sucking with startled eyes before resettling to their feed.

Their mother forced herself to relax. 'No, no. My babies are fine. I really don't have anyone else to call. I'm a widow and there's just a friend of my husband who's been helping me until my relatives arrive.'

Fadia seemed determined nothing was wrong and hurried on. 'We're all safe.' It seemed a strange thing to say.

'Well, your boys weren't waiting for anyone.' She leaned over and stroked a tiny hand that rested on his mother's neck. 'You're amazing, Fadia. Congratulations. Tilly will be looking after you today. I have to go home to my bed, and I'll see you when you move to the baby hotel in a day or two. Have you decided on names?'

'Harrison and Bailey. My husband's names.'

'Lovely. I'm sure he would have loved that.'

'He didn't even know I was pregnant when he was killed.'

Was killed? Not died. How horrible but not the time to ask. 'I'm sorry. But I'm sure, somewhere, he knows. Do try and get some sleep as soon as they do.'

'Thanks, Carmen. You've given me so much strength in all of this. It means so much that you weren't cross with me for leaving it so late.'

'You were always strong, Fadia. So amazing. And we know babies come when they want.' Carmen grinned. 'You must have a guardian angel. And that makes sense. Thank you for a lovely end to my night.' She waved and almost bumped into Tilly, the day midwife, passing the door.

'Finally going home?' Tilly glanced at her watch.

Carmen knew she was nearly an hour late getting away already. 'At last.'

'You working this afternoon as well?'

'Doing the one p.m. at the hotel till seven. I get to sleep in my bed tonight.'

Tilly shook her head. 'Don't know how you do it. I'd be dead doing those hours as well as night duty.'

'I get around four hours' sleep.' Carmen shrugged. 'It's short term. But I'm starting to come down from the night's euphoria. But I am tired now.' She did not want to talk about this or the reason she was almost killing herself. She'd never taken help from anyone and she wasn't going to start now.

Thankfully Tilly wasn't slow on nuances because she changed the subject back to Fadia. 'Well done, you, with this morning. Lucky duck. Catching twins is hard to do without a cast of thousands trying to help these days.'

'And your Marcus didn't push me out of the way.'

Tilly's cheeks went pink and Carmen felt a tug of

wistfulness at her friend's happiness. A fleeting picture of the man in the lift intruded again before she pushed him away.

She hadn't given him a thought for hours. Been far too busy. Which was a good thing. 'It must be great to have everything in your life going well.'

Tilly said, 'I'm fostering Marcus's faith in midwives. I think it's working.' They smiled at each other.

'And Fadia was lucky.' Carmen's smile dropped. 'Her friend's coming in at lunchtime. She's very quiet but, then, she did lose her husband fairly recently. There's no one else listed under "Next of kin" from her booking. Look after her, Till. We need to make sure she has somewhere to go after she's discharged.'

'Yes, Mother Carmen.' Tilly's answer was light but the look they exchanged reassured her that her friend would be extra vigilant. Tilly would be just as determined as Carmen to be there for any mother, let alone one with twins who had twice as many reasons for moments of unusual interest.

After too few hours' sleep it was time for Carmen to dress for work again. This time she would be providing postnatal midwifery in the baby hotel, a pet name the medical profession used for the five-star beach resort that catered for a few privately insured postnatal mothers. It was another warm and fuzzy part of her job and the women she supported often existed on less sleep than she'd had so a few yawns between friends was quite acceptable.

It was even better if she'd been with the women in labour and could follow their progress until they went home.

As she pressed the lift button in the car park she couldn't help thinking of the man on level seven. Zafar. Mysterious name. And what would have happened to him if she hadn't been in the lift that extra floor? The memory of their close encounter burned brightest.

She screwed up her face. 'Go away.' The words hung quietly between her and the closed lift door and she twisted her head uneasily to make sure nobody had heard.

There'd been something incredibly vulnerable about such a virile and powerful-looking man sweating over a stalled lift. Which maybe explained a little why she hadn't backed off more quickly.

There had been nothing vulnerable in the way he'd crowded her after, though. Or the way she'd almost dared him to kiss her. She couldn't help the curve of her lips at the return of that memory and thought rue-fully that he'd never want to see her again.

Which was fine. Her husband's underhand conniv-ing had taken her home, undermined her self-respect—though she supposed she should thank him because she was tougher than ever now—and taught her to reserve judgement for a long while yet.

But Zafar's face seemed indelibly stamped in her memory. Dark, tortured eyes under black brows and a firm yet wickedly sexy mouth that captured her atten-tion with such assurance—a mouth that looked used to command. Everywhere. She felt the re-kindling of awareness low and hot in her belly. Outrageous. She shook her head. She wasn't going there.

The guy embodied everything she hated about men. Power and prestige. She knew he had it despite his aversion to a stalled lift, and she had no doubt he could be as cynically ruthless as he looked.

He had to have extreme wealth, of course. The very expensive watch and the suit that shrieked of a tailor her ex would have killed to find were dead giveaways. Though why he was out in the beach fringes of eastern Sydney was a mystery.

She really needed to stop thinking about him, but once inside the lift she could picture him across from her easily, too easily, in fact, for someone she'd met for five minutes twenty-four hours ago.

The lift stopped on six and she stepped out onto the main baby floor and made her way to the midwives' room. To work, woman!

As she discussed her patients with the morning shift midwife she was surprised to hear that Fadia had already been moved to the hotel. Occasionally a very well woman with her second or subsequent baby would move across after four hours but for a first-time mum with twins it was very unusual.

'And the paediatrician said it was okay? And Tilly's Dr Bennett as well?'

'They'll both be visiting daily here and a mothercraft nurse transferred across with her.'

Special considerations, then. Not the first time wealthy clients had brought their own nurse but she hadn't envisaged Fadia being like that. 'That will help.'

'Not any more. Fadia sent her away as soon as she was settled. Apparently didn't like her.'

Carmen raised her eyebrows. 'Curiouser and curiouser.'

Fifteen minutes later when Carmen knocked on

Fadia's door, the last person she expected to open it was the man from the elevator.

Zafar.

Her pulse jumped and he captured her gaze easily and held it, just as he held the small smile on his lips. Heat flooded her cheeks.

CHAPTER TWO

'AH. THE midwife. Come in.' As if she was always turning up on his doorstep.

She hoped her mouth was closed because he looked jaw-droppingly handsome when he wasn't terrified. He seemed ten times taller and broader than before but she guessed her first real impression must have been coloured by his distress.

'It seems I must thank you for your magnificent skills at the delivery of Fadia's twins.'

'Being there was a privilege. Fadia did all the hard work. I was just catching.'

He smiled sardonically. 'Yet some skill is required with multiple birth.'

He leaned casually against the door. Funny how she had the idea he was as relaxed as a tiger about to spring.

Fadia, perched on the edge of the chair with one of her sons, looked anything but calm and Carmen's fluttery surprise turned to bristling protection of her patient.

Was the lift almost-kisser the person Fadia was scared of? 'Is this your husband's friend?'

Fadia shot a startled glance at Zafar and then back at Carmen's face. 'No. Goodness, no.' Carmen couldn't help the relief. That saved a bad lack of professionalism and would be a sorry pickle.

'No, this is my cousin. From Zandorro.' Fadia sent another glance his way—this time slightly less anxious. 'He's come in response to a letter I sent to my grandfather and to see if I need help.'

Zafar inclined his head. 'Ensuring you and your babies are well. So I can pass the good news onto your relatives, yes.' He turned to Carmen and raised one sardonic eyebrow. 'So you haven't met the elusive friend of our newest family members either, then?'

'No.' Carmen had no plan to elaborate. She shrugged to let him know that family dynamics were none of her business. 'But perhaps you could excuse us while I spend a short time privately with Fadia?'

'Is that totally necessary?' Such surprise when she'd said it and obviously a request uncommon in his experience. Carmen bit back her smile at his shock. So, we don't like being asked to leave, she thought. How interesting.

Just who was he? But it didn't really matter. She'd had four hours' sleep, she was worried about Fadia, and wasn't in the mood for tantrums. 'Yes. Afraid so.' Tough. Out you go, though she didn't say it out loud.

He frowned down his haughty nose and thinned those sexy lips until they almost disappeared, which was a shame, but proclaimed this man expected obedience, not orders.

Welcome to my back yard, buddy. Carmen squared her shoulders and fixed the smile on her face. She could be as tough as he was. Or tougher, if needed.

His eyes clashed with hers. It seemed he was going to cross his arms and flatly refuse.

What would she do then? She had no idea. Figure something out. Mentally she crossed her own arms. Bring it on. Never hassle a woman off night duty.

He didn't. On the brink of refusal he hesitated, gave her a mocking smile that actually made her feel more uncomfortable than a flat refusal—almost a promise of retribution—and annoyingly her satisfaction at the win dimmed.

She didn't like that look. Or the feeling it left her with. Who was this guy?

'I shall return,' he said to his cousin with a stern glance in Carmen's direction, 'when your midwife is finished with you, Fadia.'

Fadia nodded, twisted her hands, and Carmen inclined her head politely. She couldn't wait to ask Fadia what the problem was.

'We won't be long,' she said sweetly as she opened the door for him. The lock shut with the heavily finality hotel doors had and thankfully the room returned to a spacious suite.

Amazing how much breathing space one man could take up. Carmen looked at her patient. 'You okay?'

'Yes.' The young woman hunched her shoulders and tightened the grip on the baby in her arms. Fadia didn't look okay. She looked shattered, on the brink of tears, and Carmen just wanted to hug her.

'And your babies?'

'Fine.' Fadia glanced across at her other baby asleep in the cot and visibly shook. 'I can't believe he actually left. You told him to go!'

'Of course.' She wasn't wasting time on him, she was worried about her patient. Something was badly wrong here.

'Zafar wasn't listed as next of kin?'

'I didn't know if the family recognised me.'

'So his arrival was unexpected?'

'Yes. No.' She lowered her voice. 'I wrote to my grandfather last week but Tom said I would be sorry when the family took over my life. But I'm glad Zafar is here while I decide what I wish to do.'

'Well you have a few days to think about it before you have to go anywhere.' She took Fadia's pulse. It was faster than normal, she hoped just down to agitation and not a postnatal problem. 'I'm surprised to see they allowed you out of hospital so soon after birth.'

'They said I could come across to the hotel today as long as I brought the mothercraft nurse. My cousin visited me soon after you left this morning and arranged one when I asked.'

Carmen glanced around the otherwise empty room but didn't comment on the fact the mothercraft nurse was nowhere to be seen.

Fadia shrugged. 'We did not get on. So she left.'

'Oh.' Not a lot she could gather from that. 'That's very quick transfer for twins. Because of your over-extended uterus you're at risk of bleeding. We need to watch for that. And you'd get much more help if you stayed on the ward. I could have you readmitted back there.' Especially if your cousin helped you leave, she thought.

Fadia shook her head. 'Now that he's found me, I'd prefer to be here. Apparently the paediatrician will visit me as well. I hate hospitals, which is why I was so late coming in. Zafar wants me to have private nurses. I said I knew you and was comfortable without.' She looked up and pleaded, 'That is my biggest concern. I want to care for my babies myself, not with some nurse taking control as soon as they cry. Which is why I am unsure if I wish to return to Zandorro.'

Carmen could understand that but she wasn't so sure Fadia knew how much work two small babies could be. 'Well good for you, but it will be exhausting, even if it's a great way for a mother to feel.'

Fadia nodded with relief. 'Access to the baby hotel is why I chose your hospital. Tilly said you were working here today so I wanted to come across now.'

'Okay, I can understand preferring to be here than hospital.' But that didn't explain her cousin's agreement when most people would realise the twins needed more observation too.

'I do feel a little less alone now Prince Zafar has arrived.'

'Prince Zafar.' Carmen blinked. Prince of what? 'Like Prince Charles?'

'From the desert. Zafar is fourth in line to the throne of Zandorro.'

'A sheik?' That explained a lot. 'So you're from this Zandorro, too?'

'My family were from a small but powerful country in the desert. My father is dead, my mother left five years ago and brought me to Australia with her, but she sadly passed away not long after we arrived.'

So much drama and tragedy for one woman to cope with. But why was Fadia so unsure it was a good thing her cousin had found her?

She'd known Zafar was someone out of the ordinary, but it wasn't an everyday occurrence to run into a prince. Or be trapped in a lift with one. Or be almost kissed by one.

No wonder he expected to be obeyed. And she'd coolly told him to leave. She struggled not to smile. Too funny.

She needed to think about this. 'So if he's your cousin,' Which made Fadia…? 'Does that make you a princess?'

'Yes.'

She pointed to her sons. 'I'm guessing they're princes too, then?' She looked at the babies. 'And you walked into the hospital at the last minute alone to deliver twins?'

A cloud passed over Fadia's face and her voice lowered until Carmen strained to hear her. 'Unfortunately, when my husband died, I was alone and pregnant and the only help I've had has been from friends of my husband, but I'm starting to think I don't really trust them.'

'Tom told me I was being followed and I moved out of my flat close to the hospital into a hotel for what turned out to be the last day of my pregnancy. The poor driver was beside himself that I would have my babies in his taxi.'

Carmen could imagine it. She'd bet he was terrified. 'You were lucky they weren't.' Crikey.

Fadia's eyes filled. 'I think Tom didn't want Zafar to find me. Zafar is here to take me back to his country, and I am starting to think that is a good thing, but it will separate me from the memories of my husband and mother. Yet my sons need their heritage. Tom said he will help me stay in Australia.' Her voice became a whisper. 'But I'm not sure that is what I want.'

'So when is your husband's friend—Tom, is it?— coming?'

'Today. And I'm scared for my sons.' Fadia began

to shake and Carmen frowned as the woman struggled to pull herself together. 'I hate being weak. But I seem to have lost my strength since my husband died.'

Poor Fadia. And, boy, she was really in the middle of something here, Carmen thought. Then the twin in his cot screwed up his face and let out a blood-curdling wail as if aware of the tragedy of his mother. At least she could do something while her brain raced.

She unwrapped the little boy and checked his nappy before she re-wrapped and lifted him out of the crib. 'Don't be cross, little prince.' Then she tucked him into her neck and gently patted his bottom. The unconscious rhythm soothed them both.

She needed to understand how she could help Fadia. 'So do you want me to keep this Tom away?'

Fadia's eyes widened. 'Can you do that?'

'Midwives are very good at screening people without upsetting them.' Carmen shrugged. 'Lots of times a mother's labour is going slowly because of an inappropriate person in the birthing room.' She grinned. 'Like a scary mother-in-law or a friend she couldn't say no to.' She smiled. 'We suggest they have some time out and they don't get them back in until the mother asks us to.' She spread her hands. 'I could hold Tom off for you. But isn't your cousin better for that?'

Fadia stroked the bed sheet with her fingers. 'No. The situation could escalate more than I want'

A strange thing to say but Fadia's fingers twisted and turned and Carmen held her tongue. 'Or Zafar might do something to him.'

Carmen barely stopped herself from rolling her eyes. Oh, come on. This isn't the Middle Ages.'

'You don't understand.'

'Okay. So, this Tom? Have you got a photo of him?'

Fadia thought for a moment and then nodded. She reached for her purse and removed a photo of a smiling couple, the woman Fadia.

'Your husband?' Fadia nodded. Carmen looked at the third person in the photo and there was something about him that reminded her of her ex. Carl. A hardness around his eyes, a sleaziness in his smile. She was good at picking that up now.

Fadia was shaking and Carmen felt for her. That was enough emotional drama for this exhausted mum. 'Fadia. Can I borrow this? I'll copy it and give my friend downstairs a copy. We'll keep an eye out and and nobody will be hurt. But for now...' she held the baby towards his mother '...we could get these boys fed because this little one is going to bring the roof down if he really gets going. And you're not going to have time to worry about annoying Toms, or frowning Zafars, because these boys will keep you on your toes without them. And after that you get to rest.'

Fadia nodded and some of the strain left her face. 'You're right. Thank you.'

An hour later, when Carmen opened the door of Fadia's room, a tall man in a flowing robe stood up from the chair at the end of the corridor and stared at her as she hesitated in the doorway. What was going on here?

Good grief. This was getting worse. She was guessing Zafar had put a guard on Fadia so maybe there was more she needed to know.

They were infecting her with their dramas but the last thing the new mum needed was more tension and Carmen needed to know what she was up against.

Carmen stiffened her shoulders, let the room door shut behind her and marched up to the guard. 'I'm assuming you're Prince Zafar's man?'

He bowed his head, though his expression remained anything but subservient. 'Yes, madame. I am Yusuf.'

'Then, Yusuf, perhaps you could take me to your prince, please.'

'No.'

'No?'

'I think not.' The guard raised his eyebrows, looked her up and down, as if to say she was only a woman and a servant at that, and Carmen's usually dormant temper flickered. She glared at him. This was really beyond a joke.

Any minute now Fadia could poke her head out and see she was under guard.

Her voice firmed. 'I think so. Right now, thank you. I'm quite happy to use the stairs.' She smiled sweetly. 'The prince and I do know each other.' A white lie. Serve Zafar right for flirting with her.

She and Yusuf, her new best friend—not—stared at each other for a moment and she could see a faint scar running the full length of the man's face. He was probably extremely used to defending his prince.

There was stalemate as the silence went on and she threw caution to the winds. 'I'd hate to have to pass on my displeasure.'

The man's face tightened and he shrugged fatalistically. 'As you wish. This way.' He opened the door to the stairwell and allowed her to precede him. Carmen could hear the swish of his robes behind her, even though his footsteps were silent.

'Please wait.'

She glanced back and Yusuf held up his hand.

She paused at the top of the stairs and the guard leaned forward and opened the heavy door for her. That second of waiting gave her time to realise she had no clear agenda for her visit with the prince when she arrived. Was it enough of her business to barge in? What on earth was she doing here?

On the seventh floor Carmen could see another guard standing outside the door to the presidential suite and the reality sank in a little further about how different this man's life was from hers. And how out of her depth she really was.

She paused to say she'd changed her mind but one glance at the cynical face beside her told her dear Yusuf had picked up on her discomfort. Great to know she was providing him with amusement.

That decided her.

Yusuf glanced once more at her determined chin, nodded at the man standing guard, then knocked on the large wooden door.

A few seconds later a tiny robed woman appeared and they spoke a language Carmen didn't understand but it wasn't hard to guess what was said—something along the lines of stupid woman annoying our prince, no doubt.

The woman glanced over Carmen, shrugged and stepped back to allow them to enter.

The room opened into a window lined terrace and the magnificent blue vista of Coogee Bay curved like a sickle seven floors below. The scent of sandalwood was strong and quiet discordant music played discreetly in the background.

Several low armchairs were grouped together and

there were heaped cushions on colour-rich carpets, all facing the entertainment centre on one side of the room, and a boardroom table with a dozen comfortable chairs took up space on the other.

She'd been in this room before and the furnishing had changed dramatically. It seemed Prince Zafar travelled with his own furniture. A tad different from her bedsit with a rickety bed.

A door leading off into another room opened and Zafar came out—no, she thought, he made an entrance. Dressed in white traditional robes of an Arab, with his head covered, she couldn't help a little more gaping.

His brows drew together when he saw her but he came forward until he stood in front of her. He looked even bigger and more formidable surrounded by his servants but this time it was not only his physical presence, more the scent of distinct power.

'You wished to see me.'

She felt the pressure from interested eyes, and he too glanced around. He spoke three short, sharp words that cleared the room like magic.

Despite herself, she was impressed and to her irritation couldn't deny a little nervous thrill now that they were alone.

'Please…' he gestured to the lounge chairs '…be seated.' He gestured to the tiny kitchen. 'Would you like a juice or water?'

'No, thank you.' Despite her dry mouth. Maybe she should have had one to give herself time to think of something to say.

He sat when she did. 'In that case, what can I do for you?'

She had no idea. 'I wish to discuss your cousin.'

He inclined his head and she suspected a fleeting crinkle of amusement before he assumed a serious face again. 'I had guessed that was the case.'

Now she felt silly. Of course he did. She wasn't here because he'd almost kissed her. Was she? The thought brought a tide of pink to her cheeks and she felt like sliding under the gorgeous carpet or pulling one of those cushions over her face. How did she get herself into these situations?

Another flash of humour. 'Let me help you.'

She blinked. It wasn't where she expected help to come from but she'd take it.

'You're wondering if I am an ogre, or some medieval lord who drags around unwilling women and their babies...' he caught her eye and she was sure he could read her agreement in her face, but he went on, '...back to being imprisoned in their homeland.'

Just making sure it's not something like that. 'Not quite so dramatic but yes.'

'Thank you for your honesty. Let me explain. Apart from things you cannot be aware of, I think to clear the air between us could save us both some time.'

He smiled at her and she could feel herself soften. Even lean slightly towards him until she realised what she was doing. He seemed so reasonable and she was starting to believe she'd done the right thing to come here in the first place. This guy had serious charisma when he turned it on. She needed to remember that.

A random worry niggled and jostled with her hormones for attention. Please, don't let me fall again. Carl had been this smooth. This 'open' and friendly at first. Before she'd agreed to marry him and discovered how dark his soul really was. She was too easily sucked in by smooth guys. Guys she almost allowed to kiss her in elevators. She felt her shoulders stiffen with the thought. Good.

'By now you have discovered who I am, although I imagine my title would mean little to you?' The inflexion made it a question and she answered like the puppet she was trying not to turn into.

'You're right. No idea.'

'So...' He smiled at her and there was no way she couldn't smile back, damn him. 'I am from the small Arabic state of Zandorro that has, by the blessing of Allah, found itself abundantly supplied with oil and precious gems.'

There seemed to be a lot of those around, Carmen thought cynically, but she nodded to show she was paying attention.

'Our grandfather, King Fahed Al Zamid, is ruler, though his health is not good. Fadia's father, my uncle, was second in line to the throne until he died.' He looked at her. 'Unnatural causes.'

Unnatural causes. She fought to keep her eyebrows level. He went on when she nodded. 'It was thought Fadia had passed away with her mother several years ago, and as the succession passes only to a male child her wellbeing unfortunately slipped beneath the family's radar.'

He didn't explain that but went on. 'My eldest brother is next in line and I too have become closer to the throne because of these misfortunes.'

He paused, a short one, to see if she understood, and she was glad of the respite while she filed the succession order away in her brain.

She nodded and he continued. 'But now, with Fadia's

children being male and healthy, they are automatically next in the line of succession.'

She thought about that. Next in line? Major succession. Then he carried on. 'Unfortunately, this also increases their risk from certain elements once their birth is known, and that is something I have tragic personal experience of. Naturally I am concerned that my cousin and her sons remain safe. And she did ask for help.'

'Safe. Physical danger? Do you mean kidnapping?' This was a little more complicated than Fadia had led her to believe. If she believed him, that was, a calm inner voice suggested.

Zafar went on in that reasonable tone that seemed to flow hypnotically. 'At best. Hence my urgency to find Fadia once we knew she was alive and return her to our country before the babies' birth in case all of them were in danger away from the palace. At least until we can settle the dangers once and for all. A goal I have been working on.'

'Do you think there really is a risk of danger?' She couldn't help thinking about Fadia's concerns about Tom.

'Certainly. Her eldest son is next in line to rule when he comes of age and the younger brother is the next in line after that. Fadia's sons could provide leverage over the monarchy, which unfortunately is not an uncommon occurrence with our hostile neighbours.'

She was starting to get that.

He shrugged philosophically. 'Fadia needs to come home, at least for the time being, for her and her sons' safety, now she is a widow.'

'I don't suppose it's easy for her. I think she has some friends and a life in Australia.'

His lip curled. 'The friendship of a man who has plans to control a royal widow? A man who pretended to be a friend of her husband, who has helped her remain cut off from her family now she has no husband to protect her?' She could see the implacable intent in his expression. 'What sort of man preys on a young woman like that?'

So he knew a little about this Tom. Okay. But wasn't it Fadia's final decision they needed to wait for? She stamped down her initial unease over saying something. 'She seems to have relied on him in the past.'

His gaze sharpened and she could almost smell the briny scent of storm to come. 'So she has mentioned him?'

She looked away. 'No.' She really didn't think she'd get away with her pitifully thin denial but he wasn't looking at her.

He'd focussed across the room at the windows. 'But has he already found where she is?'

She wasn't touching that assumption. 'Is that why you have a guard in her corridor?'

His gaze returned to her but he declined to answer that question. 'Her marriage and the birth of her sons has been an unexpected development for our family.'

His eyes bored into hers. 'She must come home. But even I would not whisk a new mother with twins away until she has had a chance to recover.'

'And is that your intention?' She could see it was.

His look measured her. 'Yes.' There was no doubt in his mind anyway.

Now they were down to the real thing. Was he the type of man, like her ex-husband, who saw only his own wants and needs? Did he even care about Fadia the person or just her sons? 'Even if she's not a hundred per cent sure she wants to go?'

'I believe it is in her best interests, and the best interests of her babies to return to Zandorro.'

Controlling creep, then. It seemed Fadia's wishes were not in the equation at all. 'You didn't answer my question.'

'Again, you do not understand. It is my prerogative to not answer any question.'

Well, that was straight out. She was on Fadia's side until the young mum definitely decided what she wanted to do. She stood up and he did also. 'I see. Thank you.' Her voice was dry. 'And thank you for seeing me.'

He studied her. Intently. And she felt he could see not just her but right through her. Into her brain. Hopefully not through her clothes. It wasn't a comfortable feeling. 'I found our conversation to have been most illuminating.

'Yes.' Well, she had learned a little. 'Some of it was.'

'Good day, Miss Carmen.' He bowed and a small smile teased at the side of his mouth. The air in the room seemed suddenly more heavily scented, the music dimmed, and his eyes burned into hers. She knew he was thinking of that moment in the lift. She was too. She could feel the flush in her skin, her neck warmed, and yet she couldn't look away. His perusal drifted down and swept the full length of her. And it was as if he'd trailed a feather down her skin. She shivered and his eyes darkened even more.

She needed to get away. 'Good day, Prince Zafar.'

'My word, it is, Miss Carmen.'

CHAPTER THREE

ZAFAR accompanied her to the door and watched her walk away up the corridor. Actually, he couldn't take his eyes off her, even toyed with the idea of calling her back until he realised what he was doing.

Her shapely legs would show to advantage in traditional dress and her formless tunic still did not disguise the lushness of her body. He could quite clearly remember his view from yesterday and had even recognised the scent of her skin next to his today.

Unexpected recognition when he barely remembered any woman since his wife had been killed.

The memory saddened him and pulled his mind away from Fadia's midwife.

Poor, sweet Adele. Theirs had been an arranged marriage, she younger than him, eager to please and expecting her husband to keep her safe. Her broken-hearted family had entrusted him with their precious daughter and he'd failed. The burden of that guilt still weighed heavily on him, the picture of her frightened eyes before the plane crashed haunted him in his sleep.

He hadn't looked at another woman since. Had lost himself in his work until recalled to royal duty.

Now his task was to ensure Fadia and her sons were

safe. Nothing else. But he feared it would not be easy. That was his real problem. He feared. Feared he would not be able to stop something terrible happening. Feared he'd be unable to save Fadia and her sons like he had been unable to save his own family.

Prior to two years ago he's been afraid of nothing. Evil had arrived and until it was conquered he would not be distracted.

His eyes strayed to the empty corridor. Perhaps the midwife could help, though. And so his concentration returned to Carmen as he turned thoughtfully back into his suite. She had braved the lion in his own den. He admired her courage. And she amused him with her determination not to be cowed by his prestige. But she'd lied about Tom.

So the dog might be here in the hotel. He would have Yusuf investigate. And delve into the delightful Miss Carmen's past too. Perhaps she could help his cousin more than they knew, and such information would be useful.

He needed Fadia and the twins well enough to travel as soon as possible. He would feel better when he had them back in Zandorro.

Zafar strode across the room and out the doors onto the balcony, punished himself with the rise of gall in his throat from that height, forced himself to grip the rail and glance down. His gut rolled and he stepped back as he drew breath.

His mind roamed while he stared out over the rolling sea. If he cut off the bustling town below, the ocean seemed not dissimilar to the rolling dunes of his desert, and he could feel a lightening of his mood that normally only came when he retreated to solitude.

A whimsical thought intruded where none normally went. He wondered what Miss Carmen would think of the desert or the ways of a desert prince. It was an unexpected but intriguing scenario.

Carmen clanged the door behind her. Her favourite place. The fire escape. He'd burnt her again. It was criminal to be that handsome and mesmerising. But at least she'd found out Fadia was just a pawn on his gold-embossed chess set and she, Carmen O'Shannessy, didn't like the idea. Or him. If Fadia needed an ally, Carmen was her girl.

It brought back too many unpleasant memories. The way Carl had turned, as early as their honeymoon, swearing at her, keeping her awake with tirades when she'd needed to sleep, wearing her down, demeaning her after a year of desolation until she'd finally accepted the enormity of her mistake and run away. Had moved jobs, states, lost friends until finally she rebuilt her life.

Domineering men did not have a place in her life. She straightened off the door and began her descent. Unfortunately, she could picture this man's wicked smile so easily and the warmth she'd felt.

No. No trust, especially for men who could cool and heat her body with just a glance. So why did she want to run back and relive the sensation? How did that work?

When Carmen opened the door on the sixth floor, of course her friend the guard was still there. He rose from his chair when she appeared and nodded coldly as she walked past him towards her own room at the end of the corridor.

Made a good little enemy there, she thought as she stared past him to the rooms of mums and babies that looked out over the beach. When she reached the end of the corridor the midwife's room welcomed her with a sanctuary, which she couldn't help embracing, from his beady eyes.

So what if her room only held spare supplies? At least she could shut the door—which she did firmly—and lean back against it.

Unfortunately, the barrier didn't stop the thoughts of Zafar that followed. She couldn't remember ever being this unsettled over a man and that loss of control brought unpleasant reminders of her marriage.

Carmen pushed herself off the door and straightened the empty baby cots before energetically restocking the linen from the trolley into her shelves. Still needing distraction, she wiped over the bath equipment and scales she used to weigh the babies.

'Done. Hmm.' She rested her hand on the computer at the desk, but she didn't see any of it. She could see Prince Zafar, though, in her mind's eye, and recalled the way he made her feel.

On Tuesday, refreshed after a full night's sleep, Carmen welcomed the new mothers recently arrived from their birth at the nearby hospital. When she'd finally made it to her room the phone shrilled with neglect.

'Midwife. Can I help you?'

'Carmen? It's Fadia. I've been trying to reach you for ages. There's a new pink rash on Harrison that's a bit pimply. Can you come to my room when you get a minute, please?'

'Sure. Everything else okay?' No word from Tom, she hoped.

'The boys and I are fine otherwise, if that's what you mean.'

Carmen relaxed. 'Is it okay if I check on one of my other mothers first?'

'Oh?'

Carmen smiled into the phone. 'I'll be as quick as I can but might be ten minutes, unless it's urgent.' A little of the privilege she was used to had crept into Fadia's voice. Interesting family. 'That way I can spend longer with you when I get there.'

'Of course. No problem. I'll see you soon.'

The time Carmen spent with the other young mum seemed to fly and she glanced at her watch as she waved goodbye. She needed to arrange times for weights for those who were going home that day but she'd better check the princess first. She made her way to Fadia. With two babies to care for, she needed the most help.

Carmen knocked, then opened the door with her key, and almost walked into Zafar who again was with his cousin.

His black brows rose in disbelief. 'You have a key?'

Carmen shared her own frown. That tone. That arrogance. She wasn't sure why it goaded her so much but thankfully she wasn't one of his underlings. 'Yes. To all the mothers' rooms so they don't have to get up to let me in.'

She tilted her head at him. 'Of course I always knock first.'

Now inscrutable, his 'I'm sure you do' left Carmen seething again. What was it about this man that pressed her buttons? Normally the easiest-going person, just a glance from him was enough to raise her blood pressure, and yet his actions were almost reasonable in the circumstances. So why wasn't her response more tranquil?

She narrowed her eyes at him. Did he think she was in collusion with Tom? 'I hope Fadia is able to rest between feeds. Having you come so often, that is.'

'My cousin would be able to rest if the midwife came immediately when she was asked.'

So now we get to his Excellency's displeasure. Tsk, tsk. Real world. 'Unfortunately, your cousin is not my only patient.'

His lips tightened and he glanced at his watch. 'Then I will arrange it to be so.' There it was, his red rag to her bull.

It's not all about you, buster. 'You will do no such thing, Your Highness.' She stressed the title, more to calm her own urge to throttle him than out of respect. Was this guy for real? The most annoying part was that she couldn't let it show because drama was the last thing Fadia needed. She smiled at her patient before she turned back to the royal pain.

'Perhaps this topic is best saved for a time that isn't taking up your cousin's.' She moved past him. 'Now, Fadia, would you like to show me your baby's rash?'

Zafar's voice floated over her shoulder, blandly. 'I have already told her it is erythema toxicarum, a rash very common in the first three days in newborns.'

Carmen blinked but didn't turn to look at him. Obviously he had a medical advantage he hadn't mentioned. Typical.

'My cousin is a paediatrician and established the new children's hospital in Zandorro before he was recalled to his duty to the monarchy,' Fadia explained.

That would explain his knowledge and also a little

more about why they'd let the twins out so early. She looked at the red pimply rash on Harrison's neck and arms. So he knew what he was talking about.

'He's right. And mums are naturally concerned.' She smiled at Fadia. 'You might find that the rash moves with heat. So if you were to hold Harrison's leg while you changed a nappy you might find the rash had suddenly become more prominent there and less prominent from where it showed a minute ago.'

Zafar was over harmless rashes. 'I agree that my cousin looks tired. Is there a nursery where the babies can go while she sleeps?'

And who had made it easier for her to leave the hospital ward too quickly? Carmen thought. Hmm. 'I'm afraid we don't have that option here. This facility is for transition to home. If Fadia wanted to have the babies minded she could return to the hospital or have a relative stay in the room while she rests.'

She spread her hands. Her look said she doubted Fadia would relax while he was watching over her.

'Or I could hire a mothercraft nurse for you again. Surely that would be easier?' Zafar queried his cousin, but Fadia's eyes pleaded as she shook her head. 'No. Please.'

'For the moment we will do as you wish.' Zafar frowned and Carmen wondered if he was regretting he'd hurried her here.

She watched his face but he gave nothing away. 'I will discuss this with your midwife later today.' It seemed Zafar was choosing to leave this time or was he wary of her asking him to go. Either way, Carmen was pleased she didn't have to fight about it.

Left to their own devices, the women had the babies

fed and settled within the hour. Despite a tantrum from Harry that rattled the windows and an inclination from Bailey to sleep through the feed, finally the curtains closed so Fadia could have a rest.

'You can ring me if they wake and I'll help you get sorted for the feed.'

Fadia nodded sleepily.

'Ring the midwife's room if you get stuck. If I get tied up, the other midwife will be here and I'll see you tomorrow.'

The day seemed to stretch for ever, not unusual after Carmen's run of night duty was finished, but tonight was the second of the four in her week when she could fall into bed and sleep the night through.

As seven o'clock drew closer, she found herself looking forward to a break. Handover took longer than normal for the night midwife because the intricacies of Fadia's case involved so many layers. Finally she was riding down in the lift to the basement on her way home.

'You look exhausted.' Zafar was leaning against her car.

Was that a coincidence or did he really know it was her vehicle? Tiredness suddenly took a back seat to nervous energy. 'I'm feeling a little wired after today. Strange men who recognise my car make me even more cross.'

He smiled, unperturbed, but offered no explanation as he watched her.

She tapped her foot with irritability—not nervous energy. She wished he'd go away. Almost. 'Did you want something, Prince Zafar? Apart from to tell me that I look tired, which was very kind. Thank you.'

Zafar pushed himself off her bonnet and loomed in

front of her. 'I wish to invite you to walk with me. Even tired, you are lovely.'

Yeah, right. Lovely with little sleep. She resisted the urge to step back. A walk? 'Now? It's almost dark.' She narrowed her eyes. Kidnapping had been mentioned. 'Why?'

He shrugged. 'Because it would be good to get out of the hotel. Walk along the cliff top. What is it you say? Blow away the cobwebs? That is one of the things I miss most about Australia. The graphic expressions.'

So he'd lived here before. It had been an endless twenty-four hours but his background and history couldn't but intrigue some part of her. Had he lived here before he was a prince perhaps? A young doctor? That made him more normal. She met those every day.

The idea of walking in the fresh air before driving to her solitary flat was tempting. Let the stresses of the day be whisked into the salty breeze that blew a mere hundred metres away. It held some attraction, as did the idea of hearing a little about this enigmatic man in front of her.

'Perhaps a short one. I sleep better with exercise.'

'So obliging,' he mocked gently.

Carmen glanced at her car, shrugged her shoulders, and added, 'Or I could go home now.'

He smiled. And what a smile. The most spontaneous grin she'd seen. 'I am walking. Would you care to accompany me?' Still optional, and it seemed she did want to go because her legs made their own decision and followed him up the ramp like she was on a string.

It was still light, towards the last before sunset, but the salty tang of ocean breeze made her glad she'd ventured out.

She didn't know what made her look back—in truth, she'd forgotten about his bodyguard—but Yusuf was there in the lee of the building, watching them. His eyes met hers coldly.

Zafar saw her frown and with a flick of his wrist banished the man from sight.

He wasn't sure why it had been so important to spend time with this woman. His brain had suggested a discussion about Fadia but his mood had lifted as soon as she'd stepped out of the lift. How did she do that? And did he want her to?

They waited at the traffic lights and strangely the silence was not heavy between them. His interest in the companionship of a woman had been absent for the last two years and yet her company made him feel light and free.

They chatted about his homeland and his love of the desert until the 'Walk' sign propelled them across the road and down to the cobbled path that ran around the headland.

'I've never been to the desert.'

'It is very beautiful and harsh.' He smiled down at her. 'Like some Australian women.'

What was it about her that captured his interest? He glanced at her. Perhaps it was the genuine empathy she could feel for his cousin. Perhaps her obvious lack of ulterior motive. Or her transparent emotions that enticed him to savour her moods, even when he annoyed her. He felt his mouth curve until he realised what he was doing. He was not here for this.

Carmen ignored the teasing inherent in that remark and stamped down the excitement she could feel growing at his company. This was not good. They were

worlds apart and she didn't need to fall for another domineering man. But she could enjoy her walk and sat-
isfy her curiosity. No strings attached. 'So, if you are a
prince, do you have a palace?' A little tongue in cheek.
He probably lived in a nice house in the city.

'My brother and I each have our own palace in the
mountains, and share service to our grandfather at his
palace in Zene, the capital of Zandorro.'

Oh. She hadn't actually thought he was that grand.
It was all too fairy-tale but it made her feel safer that he
wouldn't be interested in an ordinary midwife. 'What
about an oasis in the desert with tents?'

It was as if he'd read her mind. 'Absolutely. You
would not believe it.'

'Lawrence of Arabia?' They smiled at each other.
'Tell me.'

He shrugged, amused. 'A true Bedouin camp is a
little earthier than mine. My oasis belonged to a tourist
company that went bankrupt. I bought them out when I
could have just waited for them to leave but the karma
is good. I use it for business negotiations when Western
wives accompany their husbands. Their fantasies are
always good business. Bathing in oils, traditional dress
for the meal. I think you might enjoy it.'

It could be fun. 'Are you saying Westerners are easily
swayed by that fantasy?' She was having a few pretty
pictures of her own. She smiled at him. 'I'm all for fantasies as long as I can get off when I want to.'

Zafar watched her face. Saw the dreamy expression
in her eyes change as she thought of something unpleasant. He felt his own mood lower in response.

He realised he'd like to see this kind woman pampered, cosseted, cared for. The worries of the world

removed from her lovely shoulders. Perhaps one day, when he was not called to royal duty and all this was over, he might come back and search her out. See if she still wanted to see the desert.

It was an intriguing idea he shouldn't consider and it seemed her curiosity was greater about his time in her own country. 'So you've lived here before?'

He looked across at her as they walked past the old baths. 'My mother was buried in Sydney.'

'Did she leave Zandorro late in life?'

He put his hand on her elbow to steer her safely aside as a pushbike rider pedalled past. Her skin was like silk yet taut with youth and vibrancy. He could feel the impact of her arm on his fingers.

Touching her skin was too distracting. Zafar let his hand drop. Too soft yet supple, too enticing, and he had no right to touch her. Guilt swamped him. How could he forget his wife so easily? Just two years and for the first time he was burdened with the beginnings of lust. For a woman so different from his beloved.

So why did he want to capture this woman's hand and bump his hip against hers as they walked? Why now, suddenly, did he see Carmen as attractive when for ages he'd barely acknowledged other women existed? What was it about her? He glanced at her animated face as she waited for an answer. What had she'd asked? Ah, yes. His mother.

'Yes, my mother left Zandorro when my father died. She married an Australia diplomat a few years later.'

He didn't want to think about how she'd left him and his brother behind in their grandfather's care. How much they'd missed the brief chances to feel her gentle love and support, which they'd taken for granted in their busy lives. It hadn't been until he'd demanded he come to university here that he'd learned the truth. She'd had no choice if she'd wanted a life for herself and the hour or two each day she saw her sons hadn't filled the gap his father had left.

Her face was turned to him. Not passive attention but real empathy in her gaze. 'So where did you live when you were here?'

And he was allowing her truths he shared with no one. 'With my mother and her husband all through university. Then I bought a house near theirs until I completed my time as registrar three years ago.'

'So you worked here as well?'

'I studied under Dr Ting at Bay Hospital.' They had been good years and he'd taken innovative ideas back to Zandorro and set up a state-of-the-art paediatric hospital in Zene. He'd been bitten by passion, obsessed with creating a better place for sick children, research for hope, and he had achieved a lot of that dream.

He had the sudden urge to tell her but that had all been before he'd had to hand it on and take over his royal duties.

Dr Ting? Carmen was stunned. 'So you're a consultant?' If he'd been under the eminent paediatrician, he was no slouch. No amount of money would have secured the radical but brilliant Dr Ting's agreement unless Zafar was worthy. She looked at him with new respect. 'I'm impressed.'

He frowned. 'Don't be. I'm unable to practise as much as I wish.' Such was the despair in his voice she backed away from the topic. This guy could create tension with just a word and she wasn't used to that. More layers she didn't understand and more reasons for her to be careful.

The silence had a bite to it now. Something had happened to stop his work. She wondered but shied away from digging. 'The view is spectacular along this path.'

The darkness in his tone made the water in front lose its sparkle. Such was his presence that the idea didn't even seem too fanciful. Maybe night was just coming on more swiftly than she'd anticipated?

They walked quite briskly along the cliff past the steps to the ladies' baths and onto the wide grassed area near the playground. Suddenly she noticed the families gathering blankets and children under their arms. She turned curiously to survey the way they'd come. A summer storm threatened, and she lifted her hand to point it out when she was distracted by a young woman in a pretty sarong, kneeling on the grass. At first Carmen thought she was praying.

As she drew level the woman moaned and they both stopped. The woman's glittering, pain-filled eyes made Carmen draw breath and they both crossed over to her.

Carmen rested her hand gently on her shoulder. 'You okay?'

The woman moistened her lips. 'No. My baby.'

Must be the month for pregnant women to be out and about alone in labour, Carmen thought as she glanced around. In fact, the busy park lay almost deserted as the cooler breeze sprang up. 'Are you in pain or have your waters broken?'

The young woman laughed, a little hysterically. 'Both.' She turned her head and she, too, realised they were the only people left. Her eyes sought Carmen's. 'I'm so scared. The pains are coming like a freight train.

You won't leave me?' The woman stopped and moaned as she tried to catch her breath.

'Ambulance, please, Zafar?' Carmen glanced at her companion, who nodded and raised his phone to make the call, and Carmen knelt down beside her. 'What's your name?'

'Jenny.'

'I'm Carmen, Jenny. And this is Zafar. Is this your first baby?'

The woman nodded. Carmen's shoulders relaxed a little so hopefully they'd have time to transport. 'Can you stand? We've called an ambulance. Would you like to move to the bench?'

Jenny looked at the short distance to the bench. 'No. I'm too scared to move. I need to stay like this.'

Carmen's eyebrows rose. She glanced at the roomy sarong. It was one of those tube ones held up by elastic, and she decided the woman was probably as comfortable kneeling as she'd be anywhere and at least she was covered for privacy.

Carmen smiled to herself. They could probably have a baby under that sarong and nobody would notice.

At work most of her births were in the semi-dark and by feel anyway, but surely it wouldn't come to that.

'That's fine. Your comfort's the most important thing while we wait for the ambulance.'

She exchanged glances with Zafar and he nodded. She had support. All was good.

'So I'm guessing the contractions are pretty powerful?' The girl nodded. 'Well, you're breathing really well. It's so important not to get scared.'

'I'm freaking here,' Jenny ground out. 'It should not be this quick.'

Carmen pressed her hand into Jenny's shoulder. 'You're doing great. They say fear's your worst enemy. I try to remember that when things happen that scare the socks off me. Birth isn't an enemy—it's nature's way. Everything will be okay if a little unusual in setting.'

Jenny shook her head. Emphatically. 'It still shouldn't be this quick.'

'Sometimes that happens,' Zafar said reassuringly. 'Carmen's a midwife and I'm a paediatrician. We know babies.'

'So someone up there's looking after you.' Carmen sent Zafar an ironic glance that she hoped she was ready. 'And babies are spontaneous and pretty tough. Do you want to slip off your underwear in case? Might be tricky otherwise.'

Zafar compressed his lips to hide his smile. The woman was clearly terrified but Carmen had it all well in hand. He could only observe, uselessly. There wasn't a lot he could do without interfering and he was afraid he couldn't achieve the same degree of calm she had with so little time. But he was more than willing if there were complications with the newborn.

Jenny shook her head. 'I don't want to move from here.'

'And we can work with that if we have to.' Carmen tilted her head down lower so the woman could see her face. 'If your baby is born, I'll catch and pop him or her through your legs to you at the front. Do you understand?'

The woman moaned and then a look of surprise and horror crossed her face. 'This can't be happening.' Her eyes darted around as if the ambulance would suddenly appear.

'It's about to happen.' Carmen looked at Zafar to back her up if needed. She knew an imminent birth when she heard one. Her voice was serene as she repeated, 'Afterwards, just lift your baby and put it against your skin under your dress and pop your baby's head out the neckline. The length of the umbilical cord will tell you how high to lift it. Okay?'

'Oh, no-o-o-o,' Jenny wailed, then groaned as she suddenly she eased her panties off.

Carmen rolled the woman's underwear up neatly as it appeared under the dress and Zafar decided that no doubt she had a use for that too.

He was reminded of her calmness in the lift and it was the same here. As if she was saying that having a baby in the park was no big deal. She was very focussed and even the woman looked as though things might be fine after all.

A mindset that had seemed a pretty big ask two minutes ago. Why wasn't he surprised?

He should really say something more but he was only a spectator at the moment, an appreciative one, unless his skills were required. He hadn't used them enough lately. 'We'll be here for you and your baby until the ambulance comes.' He copied the same calm tone Carmen used then stripped off his jacket and bundled it up like a pillow to keep the warmth inside for the baby when born. He had no doubt Carmen would manage most of the impending birth.

It had been several years since he'd worked on a neonate and a nice natural birth was not something he'd expected along a cliff path. He hoped this baby was well because he didn't fancy resuscitation out here in the freshening breeze, but they would manage what they had to. The ambulance wouldn't be too far away.

The woman groaned and he focussed back on the present. Carmen had shifted around behind Jenny, shielding her from the path and lifting her dress slightly. 'Head-on view,' she murmured, and held her hands either side of the baby's head. He wished he'd had gloves he could have given her but doubted she'd give it a thought at this moment.

The sound of the ambulance in the distance overlaid the sound of Jenny's breathing. All the while in the background the crash of the surf on the cliffs melded with the moment of expectation and added to the surreal, amazing, incredible moment he hadn't anticipated.

'Here it comes,' Carmen said calmly. 'You're doing beautifully.'

Jenny moaned, the baby's head appeared, and then slowly the little face swivelled to face the mother's thigh. Seconds later a shoulder and then two arms eased into Carmen's hands in a tangle of limbs and cord and water and the baby gasped at the cold air on wet skin and cried loudly as his legs and feet slid out.

Zafar smiled at the swollen scrotum. Definitely a boy. 'Hello there, young man.' Then the memories rushed in. His own son. Limp and lifeless.

Zafar quickly wiped the little boy over with the warm inner lining of his jacket to dry him a little so he wouldn't be chilled and then Carmen fed him between his mother's legs into her waiting hands.

Zafar listened to her voice from a distance as he shook his head to shut out the clarity of the past. His own joy at Samir's birth. The look between he and

Adele at the moment of birth. The summit of their expectations. His family.

Then family lost. Both dead and buried. The bleakness of loss washed over him until the newborn cried again and he shook himself. This was not his son. This baby was vigorous and healthy and beginning life on a windswept headland.

'Oh, well done, Jenny.' Carmen's voice. It was over. Incredible.

He heard Carmen mumble, 'Nice long cord, that's handy.'

Handy, he thought. Such a handy length of cord, and suddenly his mouth tilted, the painful memories receded and the miracle of new life made his lips curve into a smile he wouldn't have believed possible a moment ago.

Women amazed him, these two in particular, and the memory of the last ten minutes would no doubt make him smile for years.

Carmen glanced across at him and his smile broadened. 'Very handy,' he said.

She frowned and then remembered what she said. He mouthed, 'Handy cord,' and she grinned at him then back at the mother.

Within fifteen minutes the ambulance had arrived, the officers took over, and he and Carmen stepped back. Zafar was glad to see the officers offer towels and hand steriliser to Carmen, who blithely washed herself down. His jacket had been bagged for cleaning because Carmen wouldn't let him put it in the bin.

'You could reminisce when you put that on,' she'd said. He doubted he'd wear it but she had a point. His mouth curved again.

Soon mother and baby were tucked into the back

of the vehicle with blankets, everyone was happy with their condition, and with the air-conditioner set on warm they were ready to go.

Zafar dropped his arm around Carmen's shoulder and pulled her body in next to his as they watched the flashing lights disappear. She fitted into the side of his body too well and he fought to keep the moment platonic because for him something had changed. Not just in the way he felt about this amazing woman but about the colour of the world.

The idea of new life in unexpected places, perhaps even the easing of the pain he'd carried since that fateful hijacking two years ago when he'd lost so much, and now for the first time he felt hopeful.

He frowned. Because of Jenny's birth? An unknown woman's son? Or because of the midwife? Perhaps he did owe some of this amazing feeling to this woman. And again, outside his usual experience, she genuinely didn't want anything in return for the blessings she'd given him.

CHAPTER FOUR

'IT'S almost dark,' she said.

Zafar, too, had noticed. 'Indeed, I fear we're in for a storm.'

'Good grief, look at that.' While they'd been busy a new weather front had rolled towards them and looked worlds nastier than a summer storm.

He glanced up at the wall of cloud that rolled like dark oil off a cliff, grey and black clouds with angry faces shape-shifted as they lit.

Zafar gestured her to precede him. 'I think we should return more quickly.'

'You think?' she muttered, and scooted along in front of him, but it was too late.

He pulled her into the lee of a bull-nosed iron picnic shed just as a sheet of rain blew across the path. They were instantly splattered with pea-sized drops followed by a deafening crack as a bolt of lighting exploded into the ground on the cliff edge. Carmen jumped and he tightened his arms around her. Felt her shudder beneath his hands.

Zafar loved storms but it seemed Carmen had her own phobias. At least he wasn't the only one with irrational fears. 'Shh. We'll be fine here.' It seemed so long since he'd held a woman to comfort her, felt his chest expand with the need to protect, set his feet more firmly as if to ward off anything that would threaten her.

The briny scent of ozone seared his nostrils and two seconds later thunder directly overhead rattled the roof of their shed like a giant hand had slammed their piti-ful shelter with a baseball bat.

Carmen shuddered. Zafar's arms felt so safe around her and instinctively she tucked her forehead into his chest. His shirt was fine but thin and she could feel the corded muscle rock solid beneath her cheek, warm and welcoming, and the steady thud of his heartbeat in her ear.

The spice of an exotic aftershave, one that made her think of souks and incense, made her bury her nose and banished the smell of rain and ozone with a big shudder-ing inhalation. It was just that she hated storms. She'd always been afraid of storms.

'I'm not enjoying this thunder,' she mumbled shakily into his shirt when finally the ringing in her ears made talking possible. She ignored the tiny voice inside her that wondered if this time she told the whole truth.

He leant down and even the warmth of his breath calmed her as he spoke into her hair, 'We will stay until the lightning has passed.'

There was no sign he would loosen his embrace and she was quietly pleased about that. There was something primal about the extreme force of nature around them and she knew about the danger of reckless exposure.

She should distract herself from the storm and think about Jenny and her new baby but, come to think of it,

Zafar's arms kept the outside world at bay like a force field, a zone she was very happy to be within.

To her disgust she snuggled deeper into the haven he afforded. It was so darned reassuring to be wrapped firmly in strong arms against this amazing wall of masculine strength and, to be honest, that first bolt of lightning had given her the willies. 'Just let me know when you're ready to move,' she mumbled into his chest.

He shifted his mouth until his breath was warm in her ear again. 'I was thinking of making a move now.' And squeezed her arms with teasing pressure. His voice was low and with a distinct thread of humour she couldn't miss, along with overtones of seduction. She felt the tug of her own smile.

The guy knew how to make the most of situations. She unearthed her nose from his shirt and looked up at him, but she had to lean back in his arms to gain some distance. 'No cheating.'

'Third time lucky?' Dark and dangerous eyes were brimful of wicked intent. 'I won't ask for anything you're unwilling to give,' he murmured as his head descended. 'But I will ask...'

The heat. That was her first thought as her traitorous mouth accepted and then returned his kiss with precocious enthusiasm. What was this recognition, as if she'd been joined to this mouth many times before? How could that be?

He bent again, less gently, and the kiss deepened, became more sensual than she'd imagined, more insidiously addictive than she'd bargained for.

Carmen merged into the burning pressure of his lips against hers, the drugging assault as their bodies melded, and the rising heat between that mocked the puny storm around them. Then the coolness of his leaving as he skimmed her neck with hot lips, leaving his own trail of electrical activity where before there'd been the chill of sleeting rain.

When he bent to brush his mouth between her breasts she felt her nipples jump like bobbing corks in a sudden sea of arousal. She had to hang on or she'd fall down. Her fingers slid up to bury themselves in hair like strands of silk beneath her fingertips, until she forgot that sensation in a host of new ones as he tipped her backwards over his arm like the marauder he was and suddenly she felt like ripping open the buttons of her shirt to give him access.

Then he was back at her mouth and she was drowning.

A scatter of drips from the leaking roof splashed her hair and annoyingly penetrated the fog of arousal. Good grief. She'd kissed him back as wildly as he'd kissed her, for heaven's sake.

If she wasn't careful, he'd take her on the picnic table behind them and she'd blithely wrap her legs around him with delight. She pushed her hand against his chest and eased at least her chest out of his embrace. What was she turning into?

'Whoa there, cowboy.'

He stopped, looked down at her, stared for a moment and then to her surprise he threw back his head and laughed. Really laughed. And if she'd thought him a handsome man before, this laughing god was a million light years ahead of any man she'd seen before.

He eased her away slowly, almost unpeeling her from where they were plastered together at the hip, and with both hands he straightened her shirt. 'I'm sorry.' He raised his brows with amusement still vivid in his face. 'Cowgirl...' He put her from him. 'You are without doubt the most original woman. It is fortunate one of us has their wits about them.'

'You're pretty special yourself,' she muttered as she increased the distance between them. Where had that sensual onslaught come from? And no little peck. Good grief. She couldn't remember a kiss like that, ever. A year of marriage hadn't prepared her for that. That mother of all kisses and she'd let him. Encouraged him. But what else was a girl to do when snuggled into a man such as Zafar in a picnic shelter during an electrical storm? Not that!

She needed to get clear of this guy because already she was like one of those puddles the storm had just dumped. Wet, formless, muddied with lust.

She glanced around and the inky front was noticeably lighter above them as it rolled out to sea. 'It seems to be passing. Let's get out of here.'

He'd distanced himself from her too. She could feel it. Good. Maybe he regretted their ignition as well. He removed the phone from his pocket, dialled, spoke, and then tucked it away. 'Yusuf will pick us up from across the grass.'

'We can walk.' As she finished speaking a long black car pulled up opposite the park. So the henchman had been out there waiting in the storm anyway. She shivered. So now she was cold without Zafar holding her? What the heck was she doing when she got close to this guy? Apparently whatever he wanted.

She needed to remember he was from his own world, with his own rules. Rules that differed from hers no matter that he'd worked here for a while.

Zafar pondered Carmen's silence and staunch independence as he slid into the car after her but he pondered his own response more. What had happened? The heat they'd created between them, the shock of unexpected connection had rocked him. But perhaps it had just been his body requiring sex. Either way, it was not something to rush. As was the change he could sense in himself. Very unsettling. He filed away the fire between them in the storm for future thought.

For the moment he had decided he needed to secure her services for his cousin. And he did not want her caring for other women, only available for them. This was certainly a new direction for his usually solitary thoughts.

'I believe we were going to discuss the possibility of you caring for Fadia as your only client.'

She shifted beside him and avoided his eyes. 'There is no discussion.' Her words were clipped as if her mind was elsewhere and did not want to be disturbed.

Almost in panic? Why did that amuse him? So she could sense the strangeness of the shift too. 'That is not an answer. More a knee-jerk reaction, I believe they call it.'

'I have a knee if you want one,' she muttered, and he wondered if he had been supposed to hear that. Such a physical woman. More clearly, she said, 'I'm afraid I can't help you.'

Why was she so sure of herself? She did not know him. Still, this woman could be most annoying.

He restrained himself from correcting her. 'Because…?'

What was so absorbing outside the car that she must look past him out the window?

'Because I have two jobs already.'

Of course. She worked at the hospital. Fadia had said Carmen had been her midwife at the birth. No doubt that's why she looked so tired. The money answer would be the simplest one. 'And why have you two jobs?'

'That's none of your business.'

He caught Yusuf's eye in the mirror and his driver nodded. Not yet but it soon would be. Perhaps Yusuf already had gleaned some information.

She went on, militantly, so he had annoyed her with his questions. He suppressed his smile. 'If you wish Fadia to have a personal mothercraft nurse, of course you can arrange that, but it won't be me.'

'I was thinking a professional midwife to act as flight assistant for Fadia for the trip to Zandorro and to help her settle in.' Such a prickly woman.

'No. Thank you.'

'A week or two only?' The look she gave him suggested a change of topic. 'Let's leave that for the moment. Tell me how this baby hotel works. Do all the midwives work at both here and the labour wards at the hospital?'

She frowned as if collecting her thoughts. 'How did you know I worked at both places?'

'My cousin told me, remember?' He liked her off balance.

She narrowed her eyes at him but then looked away past him again before she said, 'I do the occasional night shift at the hospital as well as this. Yes.'

She was lying again and he wondered why. Fadia had said she worked nights every Friday, Saturday, Sunday, and worked day shifts on the five weekdays. That meant two double shifts a week. She had to be exhausted.

Every time she did not tell the truth she looked away. A hopeless liar. Then again, that was not a bad thing.

She answered a question he'd moved on from in his head and it took a moment for him to refocus.

'We have eight beds on floors five and six that are kept in the hotel for the private patients who transfer from the hospital. Most new mothers stay two to four days before they go home.'

Ah. His question about the baby hotel. He was interested in the concept. It could work in Zandorro. Perhaps even for the children's hospital. 'So after the birth, when they wish, mothers transfer here?'

'That's right. As Fadia did. If their birth was uncomplicated. And their doctors will visit. The beauty of the hotel as opposed to the hospital is the mother's support people can stay. Friends can visit less rigidly than in a hospital.'

She hurried on as if to avoid the topic and he had no difficulty understanding why. She looked away again. He fought back a smile. Her complicity with Fadia was not something he wished to bring up now.

'In fact,' she said, 'up to two other children could also stay with the parents in their rooms, and the access of the midwife means the transition period to home is less stressful than a busy ward in the hospital or the return to full household duties at home.'

'And the midwife provides what?'

'Help with feeding problems, settling techniques and to talk about postnatal needs out of the hospital environment. The hotel provides food and housekeeping.'

She shrugged. 'The lovely part here is the view. Mums can gaze over the beach from their balcony. It's a great place to regather their resources before they go home.'

His attention was caught. Regather their resources. He liked that. Just looking at Carmen regathered his resources. He hadn't realised just how low his reserves had fallen until the lift incident and the more he saw of this woman, the more alive he felt.

It seemed some time with the delectable Carmen could even be as beneficial as the solitary sojourn in the desert he'd prescribed himself. He would see what Yusuf turned up.

'That is all very interesting.' He glanced ahead to where they would pull in as the car glided to a stop. 'We are back. Thank you for accompanying me and my apologies for your exposure to the weather.'

'I doubt even you have control over the weather.' She gave him a little mocking smile he did not appreciate then raised her hand to open her own door.

He was pleased to see her start of surprise when it opened from the outside. She would learn a woman should be cared for and protected.

Carmen didn't like this henchman of Zafar's. This man with a scar who did his master's bidding unsettled her. Judging by the cold expression on Yusuf's face, the feeling was mutual.

Still, another two or three days and the lot of them would be gone. She hoped Fadia decided sensibly but it was none of her business.

She glanced back inside the car but Zafar had exited and moved to her side. 'Oh. Here you are. Goodnight.'

He reached, took her hand, bowed over it briefly and then deliberately turned her fingers to expose her wrist before he lifted it to his mouth.

The kiss lingered, with subtle eroticism, and her response to the intimate caress was totally unexpected. Still not fully recovered from the passion in the storm, his mouth sent shock waves surging back through her that weakened her knees. She hoped that explained the absolute melting of every bone in her body as soon as his lips touched her skin. Good grief.

She turned away shakily, ignored the expressionless face of Yusuf, and passed through the doors into the lobby to use the lift to the car park. She doubted her suddenly wobbly legs would be able to traverse the steep driveway down to her car without her falling over.

Her wrist burned like a brand and she rode down the lift with it covered with her other hand. Get a grip, she warned herself fiercely. He's just a man. You're just out of practice and your hormones pulled the rug out from under you.

The drive home passed in a blur, automatic pilot obedient, as her brain whirled and her eyes strayed to her wrist near the steering-wheel. What was she doing? What was he doing? Did he have intentions of seduction and if so, why? Did he want his cousin watched so badly he thought she might be useful?

Was she tempted?

When she arrived at the door of her block of flats a group of youths called out and weaved towards her. A bottle smashed into the gutter across the road and, not surprisingly, she fumbled with the lock. The outside light had broken and she dropped her keys in the dark. She hated it when that happened.

Someone approached the youths and spoke to them. Whatever was said worked because they turned and walked hurriedly back the other way. Her neck prickled and she resisted the urge to peer into the gloom at her good Samaritan across the road. Which was ridiculous, wasn't it?

She glanced uneasily over her shoulder before bending down and scooping the keys from the cold tiles. Her eyes were scratchy with tiredness and she just hoped that blasted Zafar hadn't interfered with her ability to sleep.

Managing the next four days depended on this good night's sleep before she started work at lunchtime tomorrow and Thursday, then after work on Friday night duty would begin again.

She felt frustration gather as she contemplated the unrelenting schedule. As Tilly had said, working seven days a week was crazy but it was only for another six months until she'd paid all the debts her husband had left her with and she'd be free. She wanted her credit rating back.

That was when she'd been offered the baby hotel job, which paid well, and for the moment she had her head above water. If she needed to work seven days a week for another few months, at least she loved both her jobs.

Carmen stripped off her clothes, hurriedly showered and fell into bed.

Lord, she was tired.

Carmen slept despite being seduced by her dreams, wonderful, stretch-like-a-cat-and-purr dreams, and the wisps of memories remained when the sun rose and left her with a small kink in her lips that peeped out while she brushed her teeth.

'You need a swim,' she admonished the sultry-eyed woman in the mirror. 'In fact, you need a freezing cold shower.' But her skin belonged to a womanly her and not the machine-like work person she'd turned into, even if her 'admirer' was some nebulous dream man with a magical mouth. She rubbed her arms. Scrummy dreams, whatever they'd been.

Life seemed a lot more interesting than it had two days ago and she couldn't pretend it had nothing to do with a certain dark-eyed sheikh.

She glanced out the cramped window of her room to see the sun shining onto the road, enticing her to play. She hadn't done much of that for a while either; more work and worry than play. The morning stretched ahead before her baby hotel shift at one p.m. and she decided to pack a small lunch and head to the beach.

Coogee glittered with tourists. Sun-loving mums toted babies to play in the waves and reminded her why she'd preferred to live in a bedsit here than a unit somewhere else.

Carmen dropped her towel and bag on the white sand and shed her sarong, along with the cares of the last few months. Life was too short and the waves beckoned with their walls of cheeky fish daring her to join them. The fish scattered into white wash as she splashed through the tingling freshness of the surf with a grin on her face.

Zafar watched her run in his direction. She hadn't seen him because her smile was carefree, oblivious, and outshone even the brightness of the sparkling bay.

So this visceral response was not from the emotions of an unexpected birth or a wild storm.

His body quickened with the promise of her bare skin close to his. There was no doubt this woman drew him like mythical mermaids drew sailors to rocks, attraction destined for disaster if he wasn't careful, but still he pushed through the wash towards her. Why he felt so alive posed a threat to his peace of mind. But that was for later.

She surfaced and wiped the sea water out of her beautiful eyes, squeezing and shaking her hair like a boisterous puppy, but it was the jiggle of her body that deepened his voice as he hailed her.

'I had forgotten the delights of an Australian beach.' He watched her face change from carefree to careful and the sight saddened him. He didn't know why, just that in the last two years he would never have noticed such a thing.

Obviously he'd startled her. 'Prince Zafar?' But she recovered quickly. He was beginning to think this woman would recover in any circumstances.

'We are not in a formal situation. Please, Zafar.'

He saw the crinkle of amusement in her eyes as she glanced around at the water and the frolicking children. 'No. Not formal at all.' She might even be laughing at him and he didn't mind if she was because it was worth it to see her expression become more relaxed. How strange.

'Is this what you do before work?'

'Not enough. But I'm going to make concerted effort to do it more often.' She looked away from him and spread her arms. 'Isn't it glorious?'

His blood thrummed despite his intent to retain his self-respect. 'The view is indeed spectacular.'

He needed to direct his energies elsewhere or he would pull that delicious body against him and who knew where that would lead? 'Do you swim well?'

'Better than you,' she tossed over her shoulder as she dived into the next wave and struck out for the centre of the bay.

A challenge. We will see, he thought with satisfaction as he followed her with a powerful overarm stroke that soon had them level out past the breakers. They stopped and floated. 'You were saying?'

She grinned across at him and a wave slapped her in the cheek. She choked and coughed. He laughed back at her and she trod water until she had her breath again.

She tossed her head. 'You might have speed but I could swim all day.'

He raised his brows and his voice lowered. 'In my youth I was famous for my stamina.'

To his delight she blushed. So she had been thinking of him. A delectable warning of danger for both of them. 'A race to the beach, then.'

She didn't answer. Just turned and swam, and this time he outpaced her so that when she arrived, breathless, he was waiting for her. She swam well. As well as any woman he'd seen, but she'd pushed herself hard to catch him. A hint of competitiveness he admired. He couldn't help teasing her.

'Such rapid breathing.' And a delightful sight he enjoyed as her breasts rose and fell. 'Perhaps you would like me to carry you up to your towel?'

She stood up and rested her hands on her knees to catch her breath. 'Never. I would rather crawl before then.'

'I believe you.' He inclined his head. Then words came unexpectedly. 'Perhaps we could share lunch before you go to work?'

She shook her head. 'I don't think it's a good idea to have lunch with one of my patient's relatives.'

Or for him to give in to the temptation to know this

woman more. Yet… Ridiculous. Who would presume to judge? 'I see nothing wrong with it.'

She tilted her head at him as if he were some object from outer space. 'Of course you don't.'

Truly, other people's opinions of him were the last of his worries. 'You are afraid?'

She narrowed her eyes at him and he withheld his satisfied smile. She didn't like that. Baiting this woman warmed his cold soul when it shouldn't.

'Then only if I pay my share.' Capitulation, though not complete, was sweet. It had been a long time since he'd tasted sweet.

But he did not charge women for food. He shrugged. 'Not possible.'

'Then you eat on your own.' She began to wade through the water towards the beach, not looking to see if he followed. He wondered if she knew she drew him like magnet as he watched the swing of her hips. It was indeed an unexpectedly glorious day.

'Perhaps you would wish to pay for my meal.'

She stopped and looked back at him and a small throaty chuckle delighted him. 'You're on.'

Fanciful thought.

CHAPTER FIVE

AT THE baby hotel later that afternoon in midwife hand-over, Carmen heard that Fadia and her babies were managing splendidly.

They went on to discuss the other mothers and their plans for discharge. As she took over the care Carmen left Fadia until last, because no doubt that'd be the longest visit. That way the other families would know where she was if they needed her urgently. One mention of twins and the mums were instantly sympathetic.

Yusuf was not at his usual post and outside Fadia's door she knocked and waited a moment for Fadia's call to come in before she used her key. A tall, swarthy man approached her and Carmen instantly recognised him from the photograph.

'Excuse me? You are the midwife?' He smiled, eyed her up and down, and she didn't feel flattered.

'Yes?' She withdrew her hand from the door lock.

'I wish to visit my friend, Fadia Smith. Can you tell me which room she is in?'

'I'm sorry.' She smiled at him. 'Or I could, but then I'd have to kill you.' Not the time for levity. As soon as the words left her mouth she regretted them. His face darkened and he looked even more like her ex-husband. She could feel the menace. Ironically appropriate?

Before anything else could be said, Zafar appeared from the fire escape and the man took one look at him and turned to disappear down the corridor in the direction of the other lifts.

Fadia's voice floated through the door. 'Come in. Is that you, Carmen?' Carmen looked at Zafar and his frown as he came towards her and decided discretion was the better part of valour.

She swiped the card and opened the door. 'Yes.' She stepped inside and held the door for Zafar as if nothing had happened.

His eyes held hers. 'Did he threaten you?'

'No. But he might have. I think your timing was good.'

'I hope it continues to be so.'

He opened his mouth to say more but she shook her head as she mouthed, 'Later'. He walked past her into the room and nodded at his cousin. 'You look rested.'

'Thank you.' Fadia smiled at them both and looked much happier. 'They've been perfect. They're sleeping now.'

'I will return shortly.' Zafar nodded and swept out again and Fadia raised her brows.

'Zafar was coming down the corridor just as you called for me to come in. Maybe he thought I was going to throw him out again.' They both tried not to smile. 'So tell me. They've both been sleeping?'

'Since just before lunch. I managed by myself. I can't believe it.'

'They'll wake up soon and maybe even for the next twenty-four hours will want lots of feeds. Be prepared.

Then it will settle down. You're doing amazingly well. It'll soon be easier.' She was talking to Fadia but her mind was elsewhere. Judging by the expression on Zafar's face, he'd taken off after Fadia's thwarted visitor.

It was all unsettling but as long as Fadia was not unsettled then useless speculation wouldn't help anyone and it was her job to help.

Carmen went through the bath routine and by the time they'd finished it was almost time for tea.

'I'll be off to see the other ladies. Just give me a ring if you need me. Maybe you could sit out on the veranda afterwards. That way you can enjoy the view over the beach.'

Fadia nodded. 'One day my boys will be big enough to run on the sand.' They both smiled at the distant future.

The whole shift passed without Zafar since that brief sighting in the corridor, which she would have liked to discuss, but the opportunity didn't arise.

She noticed Yusuf in the limo as she drove out of the car park on the way home. What went on in the henchman's head? she wondered, and then decided she didn't want to know. Whatever it was, his master had ordered it.

The next day, as Carmen approached Fadia's room, she could hear distressed babies and their mother's sobs through the door.

'Fadia?' She used the keycard that hung around her neck to get in. The noise dumped on her like a wall of sand from a collapsed sandcastle and hastily she shut the door.

'Fadia? You okay?' She could see she wasn't.

The young mother lay face down on the bed, shuddering into the mattress, the twins bellowed, red-faced and in unison as they waved tight little fists in their cots. Locked in with them for a moment, Carmen felt every minute of lost of sleep from the last two months. Then her brain kicked into gear.

Babies first to lower the noise level seemed a good place to start. She unwrapped Harrison, deftly changed his sodden nappy, which slowed the high-pitched roar to a hiccough, and re-wrapped him in a new bunny rug, before placing him back in his cot.

Then she did the same for Bailey and popped him in with his brother so the two tiny wrapped bundles lay facing each other with little frowns.

'Fadia. Sit up, honey. What's happened?' The young woman sobbed more dramatically into her sodden pillow and Carmen glanced around. 'What's happened?'

'The boys have fed every two hours since yesterday evening, I had little sleep, and Tom sent a note this morning to say he wouldn't come back.' She sniffed. 'I'm just so tired and I was going back to Zandorro anyway, but he was my last link to my husband and it makes me so sad.'

Carmen wondered if Zafar had had anything to do with Tom's blessed absence but the lack of sleep was definitely taking its toll. 'Of course I understand.'

Fadia wasn't listening. 'It will be good when I get to Zandorro. I'm not managing as well as I thought I would.'

Poor Fadia. And it was day three after two babies. 'You're being hard on yourself. Yesterday was too good and it's payback today. You've had a very tragic start to your family. On top of all that you have two babies that need you twenty-four seven. I think you've been amazing.'

Fadia sniffed tragically. 'But yesterday everything was going so well.'

'And today is a difficult day for you, plus after birth day three is a notorious time for getting the blues. We talked about that. With twins, the boys are hungry and feeding more often to bring your milk in. There's twice as many hormones floating around and with so little sleep of course you're going to feel fragile. You need help.'

'I thought I could manage.'

'And you are. But perhaps help from family is a good answer for now. Try not worry. I'm sure the last thing Tom wants is for you to lose sleep over him.' Though if Tom was as like her ex-husband as he looked, she doubted he thought of anyone but himself.

There was a knock on the door and Carmen's heart sank. Visitors were the last thing they needed now. When she opened the door it was Prince Zafar.

He narrowed his eyes at his cousin's red face and puffy eyes. 'Yusuf says there is a problem?'

'Good old Yusuf,' Carmen muttered under her breath.

As if to support his comment, both babies began to cry again and Carmen sighed. She wasn't even going to go near the Tom fiasco. 'Babies need feeding, mothers need sleep. It's a day for feeling blue.'

She looked at Fadia, who teetered on the verge of casting herself into her bed again. 'Fadia, perhaps you could wash your face while we mind your sons?'

Reluctantly, she heaved herself off her bed. Carmen picked up Harrison and handed him to Zafar. 'Here. See how you are with princes. I'll go you halves.' Then she picked up Bailey, tucked him into her shoulder and patted the little bottom.

She shouldn't have been surprised when Zafar did the same, calmly and confidently, and even cross little Harry seemed to understand the command to settle. He even twitched his mouth in a windy smile. 'You're very good at that.'

His look mocked her. 'Should I not be?'

She shrugged. Actually, she was surprised but the guy had to love kids if he'd studied paediatrics. She had the feeling this man could do anything. And do it well. 'I'd forgotten you specialised in paediatrics.'

'And will again, one day.' When my duties allow and I can stand the pain, he thought. Zafir stroked Bailey's bunny-wrapped back in slow, steady waves and stared down at the baby's soft dark hair. 'I had personal experience with children. I had a son. Samir.'

He could feel her eyes on him but he didn't look. He did not want her sympathy. So he kept stroking Bailey and speaking to the little downy head.

Still he didn't look at her. 'My wife and small son died in the same hijacking that almost killed me.'

He glanced out the window and added flatly, 'Of course I wish I too had died. You can imagine my horror when I actually woke up.'

Zafar felt the tightness of grief again in his chest. He wished he'd never come here to be reminded so forcibly. Why on earth was he telling her? His hands tightened as he looked down at the baby. 'I remember his weight in my arms.'

Carmen suddenly understood the bleakness she often saw in his face. 'That's terrible. I'm sorry.' She moistened her suddenly dry mouth. How much tragedy did this family hold?

He looked her way but he wasn't seeing her. His voice remained devoid of anything she could offer sympathy to, but the depth of his suffering reached out to her. 'Two years ago now, but I remember how to care for a baby.'

Fadia returned from the bathroom and Zafar ended the conversation as he spoke to her. 'You are exhausted. Now will you have a mothercraft nurse?'

Fadia looked at him, turned and ran back, sobbing, into the bathroom and shut the door.

Carmen didn't say anything. She patted her baby's back once more and laid him back in his cot before she turned to Fadia's bed and straightened it. She needed to do something with her hands or she'd strangle him.

'What? Nothing to say?'

She glared at him. Oohhh. She counted to three and at least her voice came out calm. 'Nothing you don't already know. You may have skills with babies but you're not that hot with new mums.'

He frowned. 'I do not understand her wish to be without help when she has had such difficulties.' His next comment she didn't expect. 'Or yours. I wish to speak of something else…'

His voice changed, heralding something she knew she wasn't going to like. Her instinct proved correct. 'Forgive me, but I have been told your husband proved a poor choice? This is correct?'

He looked anything but apologetic.

How did he know that? She felt sick. She didn't even want to think about how. 'Not something I wish to discuss.' Just what had he been doing poking into her affairs?

His gaze didn't waver. Mr Arrogance was back and of course he didn't stop there. 'And swindled you out of your home and left you with debts.'

This wasn't happening. 'Who told you that?'

Again he ignored her comment. 'You live in a slum area. Live alone, unprotected? Yusuf spoke to men who accosted you the other night.'

Carmen shook her head in disbelief and incredulous anger at his intrusion into her private life simmered up from her stomach and into her throat. The men in the alley. The smashed bottle. She did remember that incident. But it didn't matter. She would have managed. He'd had her followed? Carl had done that after she'd left him.

'How dare you? Neither of you have the right to intrude on my privacy.'

The wet washer of reality. Another horror of a man. And she'd be attracted. He didn't think like normal people. Never would. She wasn't sure who she was angrier with, him or herself, for being drawn to him.

He shrugged. 'Privacy can be bought.'

'Not my privacy, buster.' And to think she'd kissed him with abandon in a shed.

The arrogant sheik stood very much in evidence and she reminded herself he was just as high-handed about Fadia. No wonder she had misgivings about returning with him. No wonder she wanted Carmen to come and stand up for her. She lifted her head and glared. 'What an attractive person you are.'

His eyes narrowed. 'Sarcasm does not become you, Carmen.'

'Funny.' She couldn't remember being this angry. She sucked in air, trying to calm herself so that her words came out low and biting. 'Yet bullying suits you very well.'

Despite her low tone, anger vibrated in her voice and she wasn't sure she could contain it. She still wasn't sure if she was more wild with him or herself. A bitter exchange carried on in quiet voices. The air quivered with tension.

He brushed that off. 'I am not ashamed of my actions.'

She almost laughed in his face. 'Why am I not surprised?' She rolled her eyes.

He didn't like that. 'You would be wise to hold your tongue.'

So, she'd pushed him too far. Carmen stamped down the cowardly urge to do what she was told. Tough biscuits.

'Hold your own tongue, buster. I've met men like you before. I married an arrogant, self-important bully. And I won't be bullied again. Ever!'

She spun around and walked to the door before he could comprehend she'd actually walk out on him. 'I'm no woman in your harem. And I'm not in your employ.'

She called through the bathroom door, 'I'll be back later, Fadia,' and let herself out before he could stop her.

As she walked down the corridor to her room, anger bubbled and popped like a little lava pool from sudden volcanic eruption. She didn't do loss of control. Someone had to remain rational. She rarely did anger because she liked to be level-headed. That was how she'd escaped her marriage. Level head. Planning. What was it about this man that pushed all the buttons of high emotion?

Her eyes narrowed as she concentrated on any sound behind her of pursuit. Listened for the sound of the door opening again, but it didn't. She could feel Yusuf's frown follow her as she increased the distance between them, could admit she was ridiculously glad his chair was near the lifts and not positioned at her end of the corridor.

She should have shut the door to the midwife's room but she refused to have them think she was scared. She really did like the mums to feel they could poke their heads in any time. It wasn't quite the same when Yusuf appeared. She couldn't help the jump in her pulse rate.

Yusuf folded his arms. 'Prince Zafar wishes to see you in his suite.'

She didn't stand from her chair. 'Tell him I'm busy.'

His eyes narrowed and he took a step towards her. 'You will come now.'

And you are dreaming, Carmen thought. She stood up, casually reached for her handbag and rummaged around inside. 'Should I comb my hair?' She removed the small can of attacker spray a friend had given her when she'd first divorced.

'Do you know what this is? Paint. It won't hurt you but they say it takes a week to wash off.' Her voice remained pleasant. 'Please tell Prince Zafar I'm busy.'

Five minutes later her phone rang. Zafar sounded amused. She doubted Yusuf was.

'So I must come to you?'

'Or not. I really am busy.'

'I apologise. I did not intend to bully you.'

'Well, you tried!' An apology? She hadn't expected

that. She may have overreacted a tad. But the pain was still there from her shattered illusions in the past and perhaps a few from the present. 'I'm touchy on the subject of pushy men.' But she did feel less tense that he didn't seem angry at her defiance. And an apology was something her ex had never mastered.

Zafar went on. 'I wish to apologise more fully. And I still need to discuss Fadia with you. Perhaps we could find a time that you are not busy. Dinner? If I were to arrange a table in my suite for seven-thirty? That would be half an hour after you finish your shift tonight.'

Didn't he realise he was being arrogant and pushy again? Perhaps it was a failing with royalty as well as creeps. Shame he couldn't see her sarcastic salute.

'That would give you time to change.'

Unbelievable. Like she had a cocktail dress in her handbag? 'Change? From my uniform into my sarong and swimmers, you mean?'

There was silence. 'Whatever you wear will be acceptable.'

'Gee, thanks. But no thanks.'

He sighed. 'You are tiresome with your objections.'

'Heaven forbid.' She swallowed the hysterical laugh that wanted to escape. She needed to shut the lid on the box of memories he'd opened and a cosy dinner wouldn't help.

There was silence on the end of the phone. It went on until she was the one who felt like a petulant child. Not fair. To her own disgust she thought of poor Fadia, how much she needed her support, and relented. 'Oh, very well. I'll see what I can find.'

She put the phone down gently but her heart pounded

in a way that wasn't gentle at all. She should not have agreed.

But she had.

She could just picture herself sitting in the suite in her uniform, or her sarong, and she couldn't deny the fact that she didn't like the picture.

The last thing she needed to feel was at a disadvantage dressed like an employee or a beach bum.

She picked up the phone again and spoke to the best concierge in Sydney, Donna, her friend from downstairs, always good value and someone guaranteed to know the quickest place to buy anything.

'A cheap dress that looks good? There's a great specials bin in the boutique at the moment. I'll send something up in your size. No worries. Do it all the time for guests.'

The clock seemed to be going twice as fast as normal as the afternoon sped by in a blur of breastfeeding issues, baby weights and newborn bathing demonstrations.

When she visited Fadia the young woman seemed to have recovered her composure and Carmen wondered if, now that Tom was absent, Fadia would come into her own. Carmen had no doubt that Fadia had strength that would astound her cousin.

Perhaps Tom had played up to Fadia's emotions to keep the girl dependent. She hoped Prince Zafar didn't intend to continue the trend. Again she thought of her own marriage.

Her mind twisted and turned as she prepared to take blood from the twins for their newborn screening tests. Fadia grimaced for their discomfort and breastfed them one at a time to help distract them from the sting of the lancet prick.

When it was over they tucked the boys back into bed and Fadia shook her head in disbelief. 'But they didn't cry.'

'Because you fed them at the same time.'

'I'm glad it helped.' Then another worried frown creased her brows. 'When I go to Zandorro, if the results come back bad, how will they find me?'

So she'd decided. It would be hard here with her babies on her own and she couldn't help her instinct that Zafar was a much safer bet than a man like Tom. 'The results go to your doctor. We would find you and follow up.'

Fadia put her hand out. 'Are you sure there's no chance you could come with me? Just for a while?' Her dark eyes pleaded. 'You help without fuss. I would not be as nervous if you were with me. Once I'm back I know the older women will try to take over.'

Had Zafar told her to ask? 'I'm sorry, Fadia. I can't. I have my job here. But you will be strong.' Carmen gestured to the sleeping babies. 'For your boys. You're amazing and nobody can ever take that from you.'

She hugged Fadia. 'Maybe a mothercraft nurse from here isn't such a bad idea. Someone whose loyalties lie with you? I'm sure Zafar would agree.'

She shook her head. 'I want you. Just for a few weeks?'

Such imploring eyes and Carmen could feel herself weaken. Then she thought of Zafar. Of her response to him. Of being under his 'rule'. A disturbing thought.

But then so was Fadia without a champion if she needed one. 'I don't think I can. It's a long way to go for something a lot of people could do. I'll think about it but it's unlikely. I'm sorry. I'll see you in the morning. Make sure you ask the night midwife if you need help.'

By the time she'd written up her notes and handed over to her colleague, it was seven-fifteen.

Carmen used the midwife's bathroom to wash and pulled the new dress from the bag to check out the tag. Slashed price, non-iron and machine washable. She loved Donna.

Carmen shivered with the silky slide of fabric down her body and she hoped it wasn't an omen. Maybe she should wear her uniform. What was she doing anyway, trying to impress a prince with her bargain-bin clothes?

She shook her head at herself. No. She was dressing for herself and it looked good. Maybe the maroon fabric did plunge a little into her cleavage but that was fixed with the cream silk scarf Donna had added. The pair of slip-on half-heels were perfect and she'd even thrown in costume jewellery. God bless her favourite concierge.

At least she didn't feel like the poor relation any more.

Mascara and lipstick would do if she didn't want to be late. Carmen paused with lipstick in hand in front of the mirror. Did she want to be late?

She smiled at herself. She'd probably pulled enough tails today. In fact, she'd take her attacker dye.

'Evening, Yusuf.' The man's eyes glittered at her as he stood up to accompany her. 'I can find my own way.'

He bowed impassively. 'But I will accompany you.'

He didn't have to ask her to wait while he opened the heavy door at the top of the stairwell. It was funny

how they all opted for the stairs now. She guessed she'd
learned some of the rules at least.

While she waited she remembered the first time she'd
stood here like this. Had it been only three days ago?
So much had happened.

So much that her world might prove a little flat when
all these unusual people moved on from her life.

In the hallway the other guard, still standing like
before, watched them approach. She doubted he even
leant against the wall when he was tired.

Yusuf knocked and the same woman opened it. *Déjà
vu*. Except this time Carmen wondered if the woman
was Zafar's concubine. She banished that thought because for some reason it spoiled her evening.

As she walked past the woman inclined her head in
deference. Carmen frowned. She was pretty sure she
hadn't done that last time.

She was still pondering when Zafar's door opened
and he came through—in tailored slacks and a silk shirt.
A very poor attempt at not looking like a million bucks.

'*As asaalum al aikum*. Peace be with you.' He smiled.

Nice of him to translate for her. 'Good evening.'

'Now, why did I think you would be late?'

Carmen shrugged. 'Because you don't know me?'

'But I will,' he said quietly. He gestured to the cushions spread on the carpet beside a low table or a table
and chairs on the balcony, then said more conversation-
ally, 'Would you prefer to sit inside or out? Fatima will
lay the table.'

She glanced out the door to the balcony, screened
from other guests by a metal lattice and with a north-
ern view over Coogee it would be criminal to waste.

Lots of air space around them if not physical distance. And she'd rather be at eyelevel with him on a chair.

'Outside.'

He nodded to Fatima, who picked up a wicker basket and moved outside, where she proceeded to produce everything needed, like Mary Poppins or, more appropriately, an Arabic genie, out of the bag. When the table was set she disappeared into the tiny kitchen and wheeled out a trolley with dishes of food.

Zafar picked up a bottle from a stand of ice. 'Perhaps I could pour you a drink while we wait. Champagne?'

Something to settle the butterflies that had landed in her stomach perhaps. It seemed he wasn't a strict Muslim, thank goodness, for the way she felt at the moment... 'Champagne would be lovely.'

He held the glass and she reached for it carefully, ridiculously anxious not to touch his fingers, until his eyes met hers. He knew. And with that one glance she knew he knew. She frowned, decided not to play the game and took it firmly. His fingers tingled against her own.

'Thank you.'

He turned away, but not before she could see his amusement.

Carmen looked at Fatima and took a couple of calming breaths. The servant had arranged dishes of food and napkins beside a huge flat dish of white rice, another with sliced lamb roast. She recognised the bowls of stuffed tomatoes, a dark and aromatic stew with lime-green beans wafted an amazing aroma her way, along with several dishes she didn't recognise. Surely far too much for just the two of them. Carmen looked away.

'Ah. Fatima is finished.' He tilted his head at his servant. 'Leave.' The woman bowed and left the room.

'Now, I find that offensive.' She'd thought she was talking to herself as she moved out to the balcony but apparently not under her breath enough.

'And you think I should care what you think?'

Carmen threw her head up but his eyes were crinkled with amusement. It seemed she was hilarious, Carmen thought mutinously.

She must have looked murderous because he held out is hands. 'I'm sorry. Couldn't resist. I can almost see you with your can of Mace pointed at Yusuf.'

She narrowed her eyes at him. 'Mace is illegal. This is dye for self-defence.'

This impossibly handsome man, ridiculously wealthy, accustomed to his servants obeying his every command and probably accustomed to women falling at his feet. He must find it strange to be less revered in another culture. It must be strange when he was with her.

He was watching her. Still with amusement in his eyes. 'Did you bring it?'

Now what was he talking about? 'I'm sorry?'

'Your pressure-pack protection.'

She smiled. 'You'll never know.'

For a moment she thought he was going to ask to see her purse. He didn't and it felt as though she'd won a small victory.

It made her wonder why he didn't become more impatient with her lack of amenability. 'How can you be normal at times and so arrogant at others?'

'With you?' So he had read her mind again. 'I'm still working that out. It is novel for me. I was born into privilege, which I assure you comes with responsibility, but I studied in England and latterly Australia. You have very good schools, a school system that levels a young man so he understands your abhorrence of our feudal system.'

He shrugged. 'I understand a little of the differences between you and the women in my culture.' He pulled out her chair and waited for her to sit.

'But I am first of all a prince of my country and second a travelled man. I was angry today and not without power. Perhaps it would be wise for you to remember that.'

He sat opposite and she took a sip of her drink to fill the silence between them. When she put her drink down she did have something to say. 'I don't like it that you had me investigated.'

He nodded. 'I noticed.' Well, at least she'd got that point across. He went on. 'It is as well we discuss this now.'

He leaned across to top up her glass but she covered it with her hand. 'I need my wits with you.'

He put the bottle back and she noticed he wasn't drinking. 'I'm flattered.' He didn't look it.

'Don't be.' She thought he was going to follow up on her comment but in the end he changed tack.

He hitched the sleeve of his right hand and gestured to the food. 'Eat.'

Carmen carefully transferred some rice and a tomato to her plate with her knife and fork. She couldn't bring herself to use her fingers.

There was something erotically earthy about a man eating slowly with his fingers. Zafar watched her. 'Try this.' He picked up a sliver of something that turned out to be aromatic lamb, which she obediently tasted, but the taste was nothing to the feel of his fingers against her lips and her stomach kicked at that sensation.

'Please don't feed me.'

Zafar could not take his eyes off her. He savoured the play of light across her skin as her expression changed like the ocean in front of them. Her sense of humour amused him—she made him smile more than he'd smiled for a long time—and her anger was transparent because she made no attempt to disguise it when he had annoyed her. A new experience for a woman to show her displeasure and probably good for his soul. No doubt a concept that would have amused his departed mother.

The change in his thinking had continued since he'd witnessed Carmen help that woman give birth in the park. He was touched by the way she had cared for the frightened young woman. He wasn't sure why it had made such an impact on him. Then she spoke of it. 'I rang the hospital today to see how our mother and baby are doing.'

Had she read his mind? If she had, she would have read more than she'd bargained for. He bit back a smile. 'And are they well?'

She smiled at him and he took the gift of that and stored it away in a corner of his cold heart.

'You know they are. You checked as well. I understand they haven't seen a flower arrangement so exotically expensive for years. Jenny feels very special.'

He watched her taste the rice and an expression of unexpected pleasure crossed her face at the subtle tang she would not be used to. 'I'm glad she liked it. I am not just the arrogant bully you think me.' He held up his hand. 'And I do beg your forgiveness for that. Holding my nephew brought back the reality of my loss and I behaved badly towards you. I apologise.'

She looked less than convinced but inclined her head. 'I accept your apology. So what else do you do when you're not being an ogre or having people investigated?'

'Tsk. So hard on me.'

She shrugged, unrepentant, and to his horror he wanted to pull her into his arms and seduce her bravado away. How could he forget the pain from the past? The time was not right for that, could never be, while his role lay in the royal household.

Where were his barriers? His safeguards from creating a relationship?

He should be thinking of more important things. 'My investigation of you was carried out because I wish to offer you a short tenure as Fadia's assistant.'

CHAPTER SIX

SOMETHING was going on in his mind that was outside the conversation. Carmen could sense it. Physically feel it. Even discern his slight withdrawal. She opened her mouth to refuse but he held up his hand and to her utter disgust she waited obediently.

'And I need to be sure she and her sons would be safe with you.' Now he paused to wait for her comment.

'So I can talk now?'

He nodded good-naturedly and she realised she was in danger of sounding ill-tempered. How did he put her in the wrong when he was the chauvinist?

Carmen straightened the scarf around her shoulders as if to gather her control closer to her chest then counted to three. She spoke in her usual calm voice. 'I see her need. But I'm a midwife, not a mothercraft nurse. I'm afraid you've wasted your money on investigations.'

'You are good at your job. Fadia likes you and needs a friend.' He shrugged. 'So that is enough for me. I wish to secure your services.'

'It seems she lost a friend today.' She tilted her head at him.

'Did she?'

'I gather Tom is not in the picture any more?'

Zafar questioned her blandly. 'Is he not?'

She decided he looked lazily ruthless. And disgustingly attractive with it. So now she was attracted to dangerous men? What was happening to her? 'I'm asking you. He is conspicuous by his non-appearance since the one time outside Fadia's door.'

No answer to her question. Just one of his own. 'So you assume I have done something?'

She just raised her eyebrows. 'Don't look so surprised.' As if. He didn't look surprised at all.

He shrugged. 'It is my intention to be aware of things that are my concern.' He added some lamb to her plate.

Now they were down to the nitty-gritty. 'Then be concerned for your cousin's state of mind. With Tom off the scene she will be alone again and she has already lost her husband. Safeguards need to be in place. She's frightened she'll lose control to the palace servants and maybe even access to her sons.'

He leaned forward and pinned her with his full attention. 'I thank you for sharing that.' He shook his head, obviously pained. 'I would not do that. I have learned the difficult choice my mother had to make. I've lost my own son and know that feeling of emptiness.' His sincerity made her throat tighten.

He went on. 'I will champion Fadia and only want what is best for her in this difficult time. Hence the real need for you to consider my request that you accompany her.'

And Fadia had pleaded as well. Carmen pushed temptation behind her and looked away. There were too many variables for that course. Too many dangers, and one of the most dangerous sat opposite. 'I've already told you I have two jobs.'

He brushed that aside. 'And you're almost too tired to do either. You work at least seventy hours a week on mixed shifts. Why? For money. Ridiculous.'

See, she admonished herself. He'd been checking up again. 'That's none of your business.'

He ignored that. Perhaps he ignored everything people said that he didn't agree with. 'I believe you have holiday leave owing?'

Yes, but none she could take without a big drop in pay. Why was she discussing this? 'I suppose you have that in writing from my employers?'

'I have verbal confirmation, which is sufficient.' He shrugged that inconvenience away. 'What if I offered to clear all your debts for the sake of two weeks work in Zandorro with Fadia?'

She'd forgotten he'd known about the debts. It was obscene to have that much money to tempt people with. He was forcing her hand.

Or was she a fool to throw away the chance of a new life for two weeks work with a woman she wanted to help?

Could she leave Australia? Go to a country where she couldn't even speak the language or understand the customs? Could she trust him? Her nerve endings stood up and waved in distress.

'Well, what would you say?

'I'd say I sold my soul to the devil.'

He tossed his head. 'You are being dramatic.' His eyes no longer smiled. 'But would you say yes?'

She stared back at him. Could feel herself weakening

under his gaze. Bowing before his will when she didn't
want or mean to. She knew how this could end. 'No.'

'Why not.'

She knew the answer to that one too. 'You're arrogant enough while you have no power over me. I imagine you'd be intolerable as my employer.'

His gaze bored into hers. The food lay forgotten between them. 'You don't know that.'

'I'm not stupid.'

He smiled at her and she almost smiled back. 'No,
you're not, but what is it most that worries you?'

Everything, nothing, nothing she could pin down. 'I
could find myself adrift in a strange country without
any job.'

He didn't deny her fears. Just rang a bell and Fatima
reappeared and began to clear the table.

Carmen was left in limbo. Confused at the sudden
halt in the conversation.

No doubt it was all a part of the Eastern customs of
taking one's time with negotiations. She was more of
the thrash-it-out-and-finish-it kinda gal but there wasn't
much she could do.

Time passed as options kaleidoscoped in her head
in confusing patterns. She was no nearer to a decision
when Fatima had finished and poured small gold cups
of thick coffee, which she placed beside them. At Zafar's
command she left a jewelled coffee pot in the centre
alongside a tray of tiny baklava.

'Coffee?'

She nodded and he poured. 'Please, finish the conversation.'

He took a sip and held his cup. 'If I promised that
wouldn't happen? If I paid what I promised into your

bank account here, now, and you would keep that even if the job didn't work out? Plus a return air fare you could use at any time.'

Stop tempting me. Ridiculous offer. Carmen bit her lip. Surely he was joking. 'Nobody would pay that.'

'You say I am a nobody?' The cup went down and his chin went up. Oops. Insulted him again. Every inch the prince. Too easy to offend. She watched him regather his patience and go on.

'Supplying money is not hard. Finding people to trust is.'

She could see his point. But that was the crunch. She didn't trust him. Or perhaps herself. 'You may have decided to trust me but it's not mutual.'

He brushed that side. 'That is not necessary. I have given my word.'

She didn't laugh. Could see he meant it. Just wondered if his interpretation differed from hers. What was she thinking, even considering this? She wouldn't fit in. Then again, what did she have to fit in with? 'And what of your henchman? Yusuf hates me.'

That perplexed him. 'This worries you because…?'

She guessed it was unlikely Yusuf would do anything his master wouldn't like. But she didn't need any more pressure. Doing it for money was bad enough. 'Let's not talk about it any more. I'll think about your offer.'

To her relief, he agreed to leave the subject for the moment.

Night had fallen. She wasn't sure when that had happened. A ship with lights blazing passed across the horizon out to sea. Heading off to who knew where. Did she want to do that? Even contemplate leaving everything she knew to accompany these people she didn't really understand?

They carried their coffee inside and talked desultorily about where they'd both travelled, and of course the things he'd seen were different no matter if the destinations were the same.

Time passed insidiously. She grew more comfortable with him, though she seemed to do most of the talking. He made her laugh with stories about his internship in Sydney, and she with her midwifery escapades returned the favour, until it was unexpectedly late.

She glanced at her watch. He saw her eyes widen, and she jumped to her feet. 'I must go.' As if suddenly woken from a dream, she needed distance from.

Zafar, too, glanced at his watch. He'd savoured her company, understood her a little, wondered about the destructive power of her bad marriage, could admit to himself there was danger in knowing too much and that it was not just a culmination of abstinence. The moral issues of being attracted to a new woman, someone other than the woman he had vowed to stay faithful to, and where it led—that was what worried him.

He needed to think this through. Maintain distance. Especially if she agreed to join them. 'I apologise for keeping you late.'

He believed she would come. Probably not for him but because she would worry about Fadia. And that was where he would apply the pressure. 'One question.'

She paused and turned on her way to the door as he caught up with her. 'Do you have a valid passport?'

'I haven't agreed to go but, yes, I renewed it last year. I used to travel a lot with my parents when I was young.'

'Very well. You have less than a day to decide. We leave for Zandorro tomorrow afternoon at four. If you do decide to help Fadia, there are things we must arrange.'

'Don't count on it.'

'We will see.' He lifted her hand and she realised what he was going to do before it happened. Tried to pull her hand back but he held her firmly and she didn't tug—actually, couldn't tug because her arm wasn't listening. Her mouth dried and she tried not to lean towards him. Head down, still watching her face with his dark eyes, he turned her wrist and brushed her skin with those wicked lips. Goose-bumps scattered like drops from a fountain until her body overloaded and she shivered.

He smiled as he straightened. '*Fi aman illah.* Go in God's keeping.'

'Goodnight.'

Carmen didn't know who to turn to. She never asked for advice, something her mother had quizzed her on all through her childhood and later in her teens, but this was too big a risk without some insurance and someone knowing where she was. And she was running out of time.

As soon as she left the presidential suite she rang Tilly. Her friend lived within walking distance of the hotel and they agreed to meet in the bar for a nightcap to discuss the job.

Tilly arrived with her fiancé, Marcus Bennett, head of Obstetrics and the man who had been there for Fadia's second son's birth. Carmen decided it was a good thing having friends in high places.

Marcus dived straight in. 'Tilly says you've had a job offer you're not sure of. With Zafar.'

'Yes.' She hadn't expected this. 'Do you know him?'

'As well as someone can know him. Sure. We did uni together, he worked at the Royal when I was there, then specialised in paediatrics. He may be a prince but we usually meet for a meal when he's in Australia.'

Tilly's jaw dropped. 'You didn't say he was a prince.'

Carmen brushed that aside. 'He's a sheikh. There are lots of desert kingdoms and he's not directly in line for the throne.'

Marcus smiled. 'I think he is but not in the first instance. So he's our twin lady's cousin?'

'Estranged. Apparently the twins are too close to succession to be unmonitored. He's here to help Fadia get back to her country.'

'She's a widow, isn't she?' Marcus looked at Tilly, who nodded.

Carmen's chair faced Reception, unlike the others', who had their backs to it, and she saw Zafar walk in through the front door with his henchman. So he'd gone out after she'd left. To do what? She let the conversation flow around her as she tried to halt the colour in her cheeks.

She put her head down but he'd seen her and even from this distance she could tell he was studying who she was with. She glanced at Tilly.

Marcus's voice drifted back in. 'Wasn't there a friend involved, helping Fadia?'

'Umm.' Carmen concentrated on the conversation. 'The friendship cooled, I think. Either not a good friend or I did wonder if Zafar may have bought him off.'

Tilly, oblivious to Carmen's discomfort, was relishing the idea. She hunched her shoulders and lowered her voice theatrically. 'Or he could have threatened him.'

'No.' Carmen shook her head. 'I think there was more to it than that. Zafar has power.'

Marcus laughed. 'You girls watch too much TV. Zafar's a bit stiff but he's an honourable man. One who's had his share of tragedy.'

Carmen listened to the absolute belief in Marcus's voice and let her breath out. That was lucky because he was coming that way.

She'd just needed to hear the words before the topic of their conversation came within hearing. 'So you're saying his job offer would be genuine and reliable.'

'I would say so. Yes.' Marcus nodded emphatically.

Carmen wanted it spelt out. 'And if I don't come back, you'll ask him where I am and he'd tell the truth?'

He nodded again. 'I believe so.'

That was it, then. She couldn't not take the offer because it would solve all her money problems in a couple of weeks. She'd just hope she didn't inherit other dilemmas worse than money issues. 'Thank you. I really appreciate your advice.'

Tilly rubbed her hands. 'So when do I get to meet this prince?' Just in time for Zafar to hear. Carmen winced and looked up.

'Perhaps you could introduce me to your friends?' Zafar stood above them, quite splendid in black. Yusuf, three steps behind, watched Carmen impassively.

Marcus stood and turned and Zafar smiled with delight. He held out his hand. 'Well met, Marcus.'

'Zafar.' Marcus gestured proudly. 'Allow me to present my fiancée, Matilda. Tilly's a friend of Carmen's.'

Tilly was blinking and Carmen smiled sourly to

herself. She knew how that felt. Zafar lifted her hand and kissed Tilly's fingers. Not her wrist, a little voice gloated, and Carmen frowned at herself.

'Congratulations on your engagement. You are both fortunate people. Of course any friend of Carmen's is a friend of mine.'

Yeah, right. Carmen watched Tilly's eyes glaze over and felt slightly better that even a woman deeply in love could be knocked askew by Zafar's charisma.

Marcus filled the awkward silence. 'Carmen says you've offered her a position for a couple of weeks in Zandorro until Fadia's babies are settled.'

Zafar glanced at Carmen. 'I am glad she is considering my offer.'

She met his enquiring look with a bland face. 'I'm setting up a safety net.'

Zafar raised his brows and spoke to Marcus as if the girls weren't there. 'These Australian midwives are feisty, are they not?'

Marcus smiled down at Tilly. 'I'm living dangerously and loving it.'

The conversation moved on between the men and Zafar and Marcus became immersed in the topic of hospitals. Tilly caught Carmen's eye as they both sat down. She winked and Carmen had to smile.

'So?' Tilly whispered. 'You going?'

'I guess so.' She shrugged. 'I feel better that he knows Marcus and there's a big bonus that will clear my feet and then some.'

'I'm glad. You're killing yourself here and you've always enjoyed travel.'

'Not in the royal entourage.'

Tilly grinned. 'Why not?'

Carmen had to laugh. Maybe it was exciting to think about being whisked somewhere without effort.

Suddenly it was easier to let go of a little of the responsibility to work everything out for herself, something she hadn't done for a long time, and when she glanced across at the men Zafar was watching her.

She wondered what he was thinking.

So these were her friends. Zafar wanted to drop his arm around her shoulders like Marcus was doing with his woman. He wanted to take her wrist and savour the feel of her skin, the scent of orange on his lips, and pull her back into his body.

These thoughts shouldn't intrude when the information he'd found out tonight was of such national importance and here he was fantasising about a woman.

Such poor timing to feel alive again.

A time of great danger approached and he had failed to keep those he cared about safe before.

CHAPTER SEVEN

The next day proved hectic after a whirlwind of formalities made more intricate with Carmen joining the party at the last minute. Carmen only had time to glimpse Coogee beach recede in the distance as they drove away she was too busy checking her handbag to make sure she had everything. Her leave from work had been smoothed by the fact she hadn't taken any holiday for so long. She'd been waved away with little censure of the short notice. Carmen couldn't help but wonder if Zafar had spoken to them.

The baby hotel had said to return when she could. All too easy. Or maybe nobody would miss her?

Even Donna had said, 'Enjoy, lucky thing'.

Carmen couldn't help feeling she'd been manipulated by a force that was stronger than she'd realised. Zafar.

They'd left the hotel in two cars, which shouldn't have surprised Carmen, and maybe added that tiny hint of needed reality, being relegated to the secondary car with the twins and Fadia. What did she expect? To ride with Zafar? Of course she was a glorified nanny.

Thankfully the babies were remarkably settled and Fadia seemed mostly relieved with her decision.

Now the decision had been made, Carmen was glad

she'd come to support the young mother and help her as she became reacquainted with her homeland. Despite Zafar's assertion that he would not force the widow into anything she didn't want, Carmen knew Fadia was worried.

They both knew, though, that he would have other matters to distract him.

Carmen tried to put herself in the young mum's shoes. 'Are you worried about returning to Zandorro?'

Fadia nodded. 'A little. It's been six years. And I'm nervous about meeting my grandfather again. He is a powerful man. But Zandarro is becoming a more progressive country, not as traditional as our neighbours, which causes friction between the two countries. I hope it continues that way.'

They both pondered the differences between a monarchy-ruled Arabic state and the relaxed vibe of Coogee.

Carmen smiled. 'Might be a little removed from what we've been used to.'

The short trip to the airport passed silently and once they arrived in Zafar, or more likely his staff, had arranged for them to slip through diplomatic transfer to their private jet.

'Would you like something to drink before take-off?' The exquisitely dressed hostess appeared from nowhere and Carmen looked at Fadia.

'No, thank you, we're fine.'

The woman inclined her head. 'We'll be taking off in ten minutes.'

Not too long to ponder her decision, then. Surely she was doing the right thing. Carmen shivered as last regrets surfaced. It was momentous to allow herself to be whisked off to an unfamiliar country with people who played by their own rules.

Fadia seemed disinclined to talk and Carmen let her be. All she could do for the moment was check the babies and later through the flight ensure they were fed, changed and settled.

Carmen glanced across at the boys in their capsules strapped to the opposite seats. Two little heads tilted towards each other, matching frowns as if they were squinting to see through the hard plastic sides of their beds to see each other. Maybe reassure each other during their first trip in a plane.

She smiled at flights of fancy and gradually she realised she was actually relieved to be there, and even excited by the prospect of visiting a new country and finding out more about these fascinating people. Just so long as she wasn't focussed on a particular fascinating man.

Zafar had fulfilled his obligations and now it was for Carmen to fulfil her own. And she would, diligently, and she was certain Fadia would be better away from the horrible Tom.

'So why did your mother leave Zandorro?'

'When I was fifteen she divorced my father. She never wanted to go back and here I am doing just that. I hope it's the right thing to do.'

'Did you never want to go back at all before this?'

'Perhaps but it is a big thing to lose my new identity in a country I loved. I see the advantage for my sons in Zandorro, but wonder what is there for me. I am constrained by my station. When I left last time I was betrothed to a man I never saw. Thankfully my mother paid back the bride price from Australia so he has no hold on me.'

Carmen struggled to understand the concept of arranged marriage, something well outside her experience. Everything Fadia spoke of was new and interesting. She encouraged Fadia to talk. 'So where did you meet your husband?'

The girl smiled sadly. 'At university in Sydney. We were both studying pharmacy and he was three years older than me.' She shrugged tragic shoulders. 'We fell in love but now he has gone without even seeing his babies. Killed by a hit-and-run driver. Without even knowing I was pregnant. All I have left of him are my sons.

'I think I will try to sleep.' Fadia rolled over in the pod the hostess had prepared for her and Carmen gazed thoughtfully at her back. Good idea.

Zafar was in for an interesting time with his cousin and she just hoped he had some plan for long-term support.

They arrived in Dubai twelve hours after take-off for refuelling and the high temperature shimmered off the tarmac outside the window. Robed figures seemed to float around their plane, maybe on flying carpets of heat, Carmen thought fancifully as the engines and fuel tanks were tended too.

Zafar had alighted without glancing at her and she stifled disappointment, not for his company, honestly, but for not having a chance to at least see the airport. She consoled herself that she would see that on her way back in a couple of short weeks.

Both women had slept well between feeds. Fadia

and the boys' routine had become swift and efficient at feeding time with Carmen's help, so despite the distance travelled Carmen at least felt rested, pampered and ready for her first sight of the desert.

Mid-afternoon Dubai time they prepared to leave for Zandorro, and Zafar boarded the plane just before they took off.

Fadia followed her gaze. 'He does not even see us now that he has achieved what he came for.'

Carmen glanced at her. 'Wasn't that the only reason he was in Australia? To find you?'

Still she watched her cousin. 'And bring my sons home. He is a man who gets what he wants.' Now she looked at Carmen with warning in her eyes. 'My mother used to say a Zandorran man uses any means needed.'

Carmen glanced away from the concern in Fadia's eyes. 'Do you really think that?' She didn't share Fadia's concern. She was fine and not afraid of Zafar. She stared out the window but all she could see was the reflection of her own face. She knew Zafar's will was strong, but so was hers.

They'd left the azure blue of the ocean and soared over mountains craggy with rock and then the golden desert stretched as far as the eye could see, undulating like a sleeping monster, shimmering with stored sunlight that would cool quickly.

'It's stark yet beautiful.' Carmen began a new topic, shelving her own unease in the relief that at least she and Fadia had each other.

'The desert has great majesty. But it is a furnace by day and freezing at night. I think I prefer the sand of Coogee Beach.'

Fadia's comment revealed her ambivalence about

her return. Then she winced uncomfortably because her bodice was bulging at the front of her dress and Carmen just wanted to hug her—carefully. No problems about the boys going hungry but it looked very tight and painful in Fadia's body at the moment.

'Another twenty-four hours and you'll be much more comfortable again. I'll ask for another cold pack.' She raised her hand and the hostess appeared within seconds.

They'd been sliding cold sports packs down the front of Fadia's dress and Carmen had even managed to draw a smile at least once at the relief against poor Fadia's hot and aching breasts.

'Is it nearly time to feed them again?'

'Not quite. Both boys have their eyes closed. Probably another half an hour before they wake.' Fadia nodded and closed her eyes as well.

Carmen glanced at the boys tucked into their travel capsules sound asleep, and looked out the window again. She'd travelled a little with her parents but those happy days seemed from another century. Everything had changed when she'd married and her parents had died. She just wished she'd chosen more wisely or at least chosen a man of honour.

Did Zafar have honour? Marcus had seemed to think so and Carmen doubted she would be there if her gut feeling hadn't reassured her. Why did she feel reassured by a man she didn't know well? Was that how she'd made her last mistake? She winced. No. It wasn't like that because she wasn't getting involved with Zafar. She knew better now.

There was no doubt Zafar had changed since they'd left the hotel and not only into flowing white robes. He'd distanced himself from her, created a barrier through which he didn't see or hear little people like her.

She wondered if there'd been more to the Tom saga than she'd been told. Big surprise there she hadn't been included. She was really having difficulty with this servant attitude she needed to get. Since they'd left it was more obvious she had slid down the totem pole.

His persona of Prince who travelled with entourage, immersed in business documents at the front of the plane, was daunting even for her. It seemed obvious his plan was that she'd take the whole problem of Fadia and her sons off his hands until the girl settled into Zandorron life.

Then again, who was she to complain of that because he'd paid handsomely for just such a purpose? And she'd sold her soul to clear her debts and start a new life. As long as she didn't throw her body—or her heart—into the bargain, it was worth it.

Carmen wished she didn't feel so unsettled by the man underneath the trappings yet that attraction seemed to grow insidiously despite her reluctance. Those wild unplanned moments in the storm were hard to banish, especially when she could see him up at the front of the plane.

Her gaze strayed to the back of his head, the glimpse of his aristocratic profile as he turned to speak to the stewardess, the distant deep timbre of his voice. She felt herself warm at the memory of the way he'd kissed her, held her in his arms. Was she mad? What possessed her to have followed him to a land where his power was absolute? She breathed in and out slowly, three times, and reminded herself to relax. Calm. She was still in control and would just have to be careful. She was just feeling a little overwhelmed.

It was all such a surreal experience, travelling with Zafar. Her father had been worldly but Zafar was princely and there was a huge difference. She suspected that clothed even in rags he would still be commanding, and she couldn't deny she felt drawn to the man regardless of his station. She dragged her eyes away from him again. Drawn but immune.

She'd be totally professional, cool and collected. And she was not going to think about the way he had kissed her or why.

Zafar put down the papers he'd been battling to concentrate on and tried not to think about kissing Carmen. Or summoning the midwife to his on-board bedroom and seeing just what could happen. As if stepping onto the plane meant the time of pretending he was not fiercely attracted to her was past.

While most of his attendants had dozed during the long flight he'd prowled the cabin, had looked down at her as she'd slept in her pod, realised it was the first time he was privy to that view and vowed to himself he would have at least one night where he could drink his fill of the sight.

He could picture her now, her thick lashes curled on her cheek, that beautiful mouth soft in repose instead of militant the way he often saw it. The blanket, fallen to her waist, had left her vulnerable, but that strangely only made him lift it to cover her. Not like him at all.

He smiled at the memory and then other memories flickered like an old-fashioned movie. That first drift of orange blossom from her skin in the lift. They said that scent was the only true memory. He could very easily remember that first glance of hers, a basic recognition he hadn't been able to deny, and that wild kiss in the storm had rocked him. He remembered that with clarity.

Then the cameo moment she'd hugged the woman in the park—imparting her strength to her like she had to him during his weakness in the elevator, a moment he still didn't understand.

Interesting, phobia-wise, this morning when he'd unconsciously pressed the button and descended to check out of his suite. It seemed that his aversion to lifts had been put to rest. Because of her? Or because he was moving on and creating new moments of life instead of dwelling on death? Even his fear of heights had receded a little.

Not huge events but remarkable and requiring thought.

Still, there remained a lot on his mind. Fadia's ability to settle in Zandorro, the kidnap attempt Yusuf had discovered with Fadia's 'friend' just a weakling pawn in a larger plan. He'd quashed that risk but information had gained that put his grandfather—in fact, his entire family—at risk as well.

Yet a corner of his mind had been building with anticipation for the moment he had Carmen in his country, his palace, the chance to show her the sights and sounds and scents of Zandorro. To see her smile.

Normally he worked right through these flights.

'Can I get you anything, Excellency?' Yusuf hovered.

'No. Rest yourself.' Yusuf nodded and subsided but

when Zafar glanced once more at Carmen he noticed his manservant's eyes follow his.

Another memory clicked. She was right. She was not a favourite with his man. He would need to watch that. He fixed his gaze on Yusuf's face and spoke softly and clearly. 'But I will hold you personally responsible if she is not happy in the palace.'

Inscrutable, Yusuf nodded. His man had allies in the palace but Zafar had many more.

They landed not long before the sun set above the surrounding mountains outside the main city. The waiting limousines, complete with baby capsules, whisked them through several miles of desert hills to the massive gates and into the turreted city tucked behind a towering stone wall.

Dark faces peered at them from doorways as the vehicles climbed curved alleys and Carmen acknowledged with a sinking heart it would be difficult to find the way out again. She turned away from the window. That was okay. Really it was. She would be fine. She'd be able to leave any time she wanted. Zafar had promised.

Thankfully she was distracted as they rounded a bend and there ahead of them shone the palace as if positioned to receive the final light in the country through a break in the mountains. She couldn't help her indrawn breath.

Rooftops shimmered in a blanket of precious metal vying for space in the skyline with domes, towers and minarets reflecting the sun. Golden turrets glistened and one soaring tower in the middle with arched windows and a spire that reached for the sky watched over all.

'It's beautiful. Look at that tower.'

Fadia actually smiled at her enthusiasm. 'Yes, it is lovely.' They both glanced again at the magnificent building.

Harrison stirred and yawned and Bailey opened his eyes and blinked. Even Fadia's tiny sons seemed touched by the moment.

'Your babies sense something's happening.' Carmen leant over and patted their blankets but it was unnecessary. The boys didn't cry. Just lay in their capsules awake and alert as their car pulled up behind Prince Zafar's and a solemn manservant, accompanied by two older men, opened their door.

Two older women stood behind the men and Carmen could only guess they were there to help with the babies. The castle steps loomed away to the huge front door at the top and a long line of servants stood waiting to catch a glimpse of the royal heirs.

'You take Bailey, I'm taking Harrison.' Fadia had decided no stranger would carry her boys and Carmen was glad to see her eyes brighten with intent. 'They can take the bags.'

Carmen obligingly leaned across and extricated Harrison from his capsule and handed him to his mother then lifted Bailey for herself. 'No problem.'

'How did my cousins and their mother travel?' More softly. 'And you?' Zafar stood outside the car, waiting for them to alight. He was looking at her, not the others, and she could feel her cheeks warm.

Had he grown taller again or was it just the backdrop of the palace that made him seem larger than life? He was waiting.

'We travelled well.' He didn't look convinced. 'We were very comfortable.

'I am sorry I did not speak to you.' His cynical smile lifted the hair on her arms. 'I had things on my mind.'

His scrutiny pinked her cheeks more. Maybe she was wrong and she wasn't invisible. She felt herself blush and frowned at him.

He nodded. 'We will discuss this later. Rest today. We visit the King tomorrow.' He moved away to be greeted by the dignitaries lined above them.

Carmen looked across at Fadia, who was only now alighting, and the young mum's wary mood seemed improved by the excitement of their arrival. Perhaps she'd have a chance to talk to Zafar about that later. For the moment it seemed they had to run the gauntlet of the stares.

To Carmen's relief they were whisked in a huddle past the greeting party and into the palace while Zafar remained behind. Carmen wondered just how powerful this man was.

Carmen, Fadia and the boys were shown to a whole wing of the palace that had been turned over to them. Carmen's room was sumptuously decorated, pleasantly cool, and looked out over a tiled courtyard graced by a tinkling fountain. It was much grander than she had anticipated and with a sinking feeling she realised how small her voice would be amongst these people who didn't have to speak in her language if they didn't want to. Just what had she got herself into?

Then she straightened her shoulders. Not the right attitude if she wanted to help Fadia keep control of her boys and her life. And that was why she was there.

She thought wryly that she'd never had a room so

huge or opulent. The boys' room took up almost a quar-
ter of their floor, nestled as it was between those of the
two women.

A maidservant dressed in flowing chiffon pants and
overshirt bowed and offered to put away her clothes.
Carmen glanced down at the one small case she'd
brought and shook her head with a smile. 'I think I'll
manage, thank you.'

She knew her few toiletries would be lost in the mar-
ble bathroom and her clothes would hang pitifully in
the cavernous walk-in closet. She needed to remember
they'd all fit back perfectly into her one-bedroom flat
when she went home. A much-needed dose of reality.

When she crossed the expanse of the room to peer
into the closet there were half a dozen silk camisoles
in varying lengths, sleeveless, short-sleeved and long-,
all loose with matching trousers in soft shades of blue
and green and lemon, and even a longer black version.

'His Excellency said you may wish for more comfortable clothes. Until the palace seamstress has your
measurements she has sent up these.' The girl cast an
expert eye over Carmen. 'I'm sure they will look very
pretty.'

'I'll probably wear my own clothes.'

The young girl smiled and bowed her head. 'As
madam wishes. Excellency said it is the young nurse-
maids who will help so it is I and my sister who will
be your assistants whenever you wish for the young
princes.'

'Thank you. I will tell Princess Fadia.'

When the girl left Carmen peered through the open
door to the boys' room where Harrison was yawning
and Bailey lay wide awake in his huge cot. Her feet sank

into the luxurious carpets that overlaid each other like pools of shimmering colour. It seemed sacrilegious to walk on them.

'At least you boys can spend a bit of time lying next to each other. Your beds are huge.'

Deftly she undid Bailey's nappy and popped him in Harry's bed unwrapped and legs kicking while she did the same for his brother. Then she laid them side by side and watched them turn their heads towards each other. Harry touched Bailey's face and Bailey seemed to smile as Harry kicked him.

Fadia's room door opened and the new mum came in. She looked tired but a small smile lit her face as she saw her boys together.

Carmen gently drew her over to the boys. 'Look. I swear your sons are more handsome every day. And there's only us here and two young girls who will do as you wish. Everything will work out perfectly.'

'I hope so. I'm glad you're here but when you go I will be alone. I hope they won't marry me off like a parcel.' She clutched Carmen's sleeve. 'I miss my husband. I miss my life.'

So Fadia was feeling the weight of the palace too. 'Of course you do. But perhaps for now this is better than being alone on the other side of the world. Anything could happen to you there.'

The girl nodded. 'My boys are safe. That is good.'

'Zafar promised you would have choice in your future. I believe him.' He hugged her. 'You're a wonderful mother. Your husband must be smiling at your beautiful boys.'

'I agree.'

They both turned at the unexpected empathy from

Zafar as he entered the boys' room and crossed to Fadia. Kiri, the maid, followed him with a tray of light refreshments. 'I am sorry for your loss, Fadia, and know it is hard for you to come back here.'

Fadia turned tear-filled eyes towards him and nodded. 'We will see how good your word is.'

Carmen winced and glanced at him, not sure what he would do. She couldn't help feeling uneasy. It was blatant disrespect for his authority—in public—and the maid's gasp ensured that more than those in the room would hear of it.

Since her arrival she'd become more aware by the hour of the difference in power in the palace. From what the maid had said, Zafar's authority seemed almost as great as his grandfather's and at this moment his face seemed chiselled from the same stone as the mountains she'd seen on the way in. His eyes narrowed as he watched his cousin escape.

Unable to stop herself, Carmen dived into the breach of protocol. 'She's been away from Zandorro a long time. Of course she is upset about being here.'

He raised haughty eyebrows then clapped his hands and the maid ran from the room. He turned back to Carmen. 'She does not need your championing. She is as royal as I.' His brows dropped lower. 'Why look at me like that? As if I would throw her in irons?'

She couldn't help being a little relieved that had been said out loud. 'You should see your own face in the mirror. Pretty scary.'

To her surprise he smiled, though grimly. 'First I am a cowboy and now I have a scary face? You are the strangest woman.'

'No. Just different.'

'No doubt of that.' Zafar strode to the window and then turned back to her, exasperated. 'You of all people should realise I am a civilised man.'

'I'm sorry.' She smiled. It had been a silly thought. 'Thank you. It's reassuring. But this place can be a little overpowering...' she glanced around and then back at him ruefully '...and I don't like the feeling of being overpowered.'

He shook his head and the last of his anger faded from his face as he crossed the room until he stood a few feet in front of her. 'I do not fully understand you, Carmen, but I doubt the strength of an empire could overpower you if you felt strongly enough.'

Did this man really think that about her? It was a hefty compliment out of nowhere and she couldn't help the glow it left her with.

'Once I was overpowered, and I vowed I would not let that happen again.'

He nodded and she felt he really did understand. 'That has made you strong. I respect that.' He went on. 'Tomorrow, when we return from my grandfather's audience, and after the boys are fed, Kiri can mind them for an hour or two while I take you both for a tour. It will be good to remind Fadia how beautiful Zandarro can be. Help her to settle in.'

'That sounds sensible.'

He didn't look pleased at her response. 'I had hoped it would be less sensible and more enjoyable?'

Despite his flippant comment, he still seemed to be worried about something and she hoped it was nothing Fadia should know. 'And when she has settled, you promise not to arrange a marriage for her.'

He looked past her and his voice dropped. 'You may

not think so but I do feel her pain. The loss of loved ones.'

He lifted his head and stared at her as if determined to say the words to her face. 'I buried my son. Prepared his body and laid him on his side with my own hands, facing Mecca in the warm earth. I knew then I could never face the fear of that loss again. Could not face the failure of keeping those I love safe. Who am I to ask another to do the same?' His voice dropped. 'Of course I understand.'

She believed him. But it hurt, when it shouldn't matter to her at all, to see him still so badly wounded by his past. 'I'm glad.'

'I will do what I can. But she should know I do not have the final say.'

She let her breath out with relief. 'She's no girl now. She's a widow with children. And a princess. Life has been hard on her but she is strong. She just needs time.'

He sighed. 'Again it is not I who has to give her time. Already there has been some talk of an alliance for her. Our grandfather believes the sooner she has a man to care for the better she will be. I have disagreed and believe I will prevail. He is not an unreasonable man. We are to discuss it again tomorrow morning before the audience.'

Ouch, but still, Carmen thought, with Zafar on her side Fadia would have a strong champion. She had faith in him, unsure where such faith had come from, but didn't doubt his intent to protect his cousin.

She shook her head and crossed to the boys. 'She says she feels safe here. I hope that's true.'

'As she should. We discovered her Tom had hoped to hide Fadia away while he bargained with me for her whereabouts. He was part of a cell that seeks to bring down our government.'

She couldn't say she was surprised but it gave her the shivers to hear it out loud. 'He's not my Tom. I barely met him.'

He raised his brows at her. 'But you would have hidden their plans from me.'

'Not hidden.' But perhaps she would not have tried to prevent Fadia if she had wanted to run away.

He shook his head at her foolishness. 'You do not understand. It is different here. Risks are greater. I believe Fadia's husband's death was no accident. What if she was expected to die with him?'

And Tom had been in on that? Who were these people they could discuss death and murder so easily? 'So you didn't pay him off?'

'It was suggested he leave my cousin alone. But I believe we have not seen the last of his family. They are eager for a chance at the kingdom.'

She was coming to understand that. 'But what if Fadia decides to return to Australia?'

He dragged an exasperated hand through his hair. 'For the moment she needs to stay here.'

'You can't make her stay if she's unhappy.'

'A woman's view.' He looked away and again she felt there was something he was keeping from her. 'Now, I do not know why I am discussing this with you.'

She straightened. 'Because I'll tell you the truth when everyone else is too scared to.'

'That's right, Carmen.' The way he said her name lifted the hairs on her neck. His words were gentle but his eyes darkened as he closed the gap between them. 'You are not afraid of me.'

Just a tinge of danger and perhaps she should choose her next words a little more carefully. It was different here. Marcus had suggested she tread carefully until she understood the culture more. She should have listened. Zafar wasn't finished.

'Not afraid from the first moment we met, were you?'

And suddenly it was back. That tension between them, like the glow from a hundred candles slowly lighting a room, like a storm overhead in a picnic shed, a moment in a lift, the brush of his lips on the inside of her wrist. 'But, then, you have not been in Zandorro long enough to learn our ways.'

CHAPTER EIGHT

HE'D made her uneasy. Zafar understood her more than she realised, had learnt a lot while he'd attended university in Sydney about Western women, had enjoyed the company of many before he'd married. But this woman was different.

He could see her zeal for her work, her integrity, and most of all he could see the fire within her. Perhaps a fire she had no idea she held or the passionate woman she could become for the right man. A fire that matched his in a way he had not expected.

He watched her search for words to lessen this pressure between them and it amused him that she who lived by defusing tension had momentarily lost her touch. Bravado was all she had left.

'No. I'm not afraid of you.' She only just held eye contact and they both knew it a lie. 'You were the one who said the strength of an empire would not overpower me if I felt strongly enough. I do feel strongly about protecting Fadia. That's why I'm here.' Her voice remained firm—on the outside anyway.

He stepped closer. 'Perhaps you should be. Afraid of me.' A slow, leisurely perusal of her—head to foot—her posture taut with defiance, and he wondered just how angry he could make her, and what would happen if he did. 'Are you not here for the money?'

Her eyes flashed. 'Apparently money was the only way you could get me here!' There it was. So she had given up holding her tongue.

He watched her regret the words as soon as they left her mouth. What had happened to the usually placid Carmen? It seemed he did something to her too. Incited her. Well, she incited him, and he could barely keep his hands by his sides with the need to pull her against him and quieten that mouth of hers with his.

She hurried into speech. Aware of more peril now. Happy to clutch at any straw to avert a difficult situation. 'Your friend, Marcus, said you were a man of honour.'

'That was in Australia.' His eyes travelled over her again with deliberate scrutiny, watched the pink rise in her neck, watched her lick her lips for the taste of danger. 'We are not in your country now. Here honour and law interchange. Here my word is law.'

He closed the last space between them, captured her gaze with his and held it with the easy power of generations of royalty.

Carmen could feel her heart pound. He'd stopped a hairsbreadth away, just short of the fabric of her shirt, fabric she could suddenly feel caress her breasts as she breathed in and out more quickly to calm the agitation caused by his invasion of her space.

'Your law is not my law.' Some foolish pride, some devil inside, refused to allow her to step back.

His voice hardened. Became emphatic. 'You are in Zandorro now. It is my law.' Then softly, 'Come here.'

She blinked. Was he kidding? 'I doubt I could get

much closer without bumping into you.' And some evil twin inside urged her into his arms. She wasn't sure who was the more dangerous to her safety—him or her inner temptress.

He raised his brows. 'Indeed.'

She could feel the aura between them. The air shimmered, thick with vibration that wasn't all words and power struggle, more at stake here than pride and stubbornness. Her brain screamed of danger and her body dared her to walk into him. Give in. Submit.

She unstuck her tongue from the roof of her mouth. 'You might be living under ancient rule but I am not.' She stepped back. She met his eyes unflinchingly and then, to her eternal gratitude, Harrison cried. Actually, almost lifted the roof of the palace with his demands. Thank you, dear, dear baby Harry.

She took the few steps to the ornate cradle, picked up the baby and lifted him like a shield. 'If you'll excuse me, Prince Zafar—' her voice was very dry '—I will take Prince Harrison to his mother.'

He watched her, even with a glimmer of a smile,and nodded once. 'We will return to this subject another time.'

'I don't think so.' She said it as she walked away but she had no doubt he had heard her and she could feel his eyes on her back until the swish of his robes told her he was gone.

She looked back and the room was empty. She leant heavily against the doorframe with a sigh of relief and clutched the baby. What had she fallen into? Just how reliable was his honour? And how reliable would hers be if he took her into his arms again?

* * *

Zafar walked away. He was annoyed with Carmen, annoyed with himself for playing cat and mouse and having a ridiculous argument when what he wanted to do was feel again the rapport they'd had in the park in Australia. All he'd succeeded in doing was alienating her. Of course she was there to stand up for Fadia if she thought her badly done by. What did he expect?

But he was doing the best he could. Had used all his persuasive powers with his grandfather. He would just have to try harder for Fadia. And be more patient with Carmen—and with himself.

Fadia went to bed early. Carmen decided bed was a safe place, a haven, and a good option for herself as well. She didn't sleep well.

The next morning after breakfast she received a message via Yusuf that Prince Zafar wished to see her. The manservant and the midwife eyed each other and she thought of her little can of dye. Yusuf smiled grimly.

She was taken to the library off the huge tiled entry and through a massive studded door. The room had long, arched windows that opened onto a terrace and inner courtyard with the largest fountain she'd seen yet. The tinkling of falling drops filled the room with a background symphony as she crossed more carpets that shimmered and glowed like pools of coloured light, each more beautiful than the last. At the back of the room ceiling-high bookshelves circled the wall.

It could have been an overpowering room with murals and giant urns, except none seemed to have the magnificence of the man standing front of her in full traditional robes. He suited the room too well.

'How did you sleep?'

How did he think? After the first two hours it had taken her to banish their last encounter. 'Fine, thank you.'

'And the boys?' So he was to be solicitous this morning?

She answered calmly. 'We have a routine. Necessary with twins that are breastfed. They sleep longer at night.'

Still he watched her. Did she have a smut on her nose? 'And they are growing well.'

She glanced around the room, looking for clues to this conversation. 'They certainly seem to be. I don't have scales but as long as they're giving us plenty of wet nappies a day, they're fine.

He nodded decisively. 'I will have scales sent to the nursery.'

'As you wish.'

He allowed himself a small smile. 'Now, was that so hard to say?'

She glared at him. 'Am I allowed to ask what happened with your communication with the King this morning?'

'The king has agreed to leave Fadia in my hands for the moment. Which is why I have summoned you.'

She let him get away with summoned because this was much more serious. 'Does she know?'

'I will inform her this afternoon before our audience.' He walked to the window and looked out. 'We meet to postpone our tour tomorrow. Of necessity our time away from the boys will be short. I wish to know if you have a preference for the souks or a drive around the city to see a broader example of the sights?'

'Perhaps the sights, and at least then I may understand the city better.'

'As you wish. The city, then. Taqu, my friend, wishes to accompany us. Do you mind?'

'Why should I mind? But I'm not sure about Fadia. Does she know him?'

'No. Though he was originally betrothed to Fadia before her mother left. He is a good man and wishes to see her.'

'So at least she knows him?'

'They have never formally met and since then he did marry but is now a widower like myself.'

'So he's the one her mother returned the bride price for? Is this a trick to have them meet?'

'What little faith you have in me.' She did have yesterday. Before their discussion.

Then he calmly said, 'No. This allows my grandfather some face and to take pressure off Fadia.'

'What's he like? What makes you think she'd even talk to him?'

'He is not old or unsavoury.' He smiled as he turned back to face her. 'Though, in fact, as a friend of mine, perhaps he is a little old in my cousin's eyes.'

She had to smile back. 'Not too old, then.'

'My thanks. Prince Taqu lost his wife in childbirth, which for someone in our profession is perhaps just as horrific as a hijack.'

Her breath sighed out. She wondered where Zafar's tragic hijack had happened but she should be thinking of Taqu and his loss. 'I'm sorry to hear that.' She watched his face. 'When you say "our profession", is Prince Taqu a doctor too?'

'He is. But I was referring to your midwifery as well.

Taqu has taken over the running of my children's hospital. He also has a young daughter who needs a mother and he knows Fadia is a kind woman.'

Carmen's brain connected to the next thought. 'Should the unlikely happen, and Fadia and this Taqu fall in love and marry, then have children, doesn't that mean you will be further from the throne? Fadia's new husband would act as guardian of her sons, and your brother Prince Regent until Harry comes of age?'

'That is correct.'

'And you don't mind?'

'Not at all. It places me another step further from the throne. A step closer to return to my work. Zandorro has already lost a future king. Now, when the time comes, if Fadia does not remarry, my brother will act as regent until Harrison is fit to be king in his twentieth year. When Harrison has children then I am further removed.'

'Don't you want to be ruler?'

He shook his head. 'It was never my place. If my country needs me I will be there, of course, but I long to return to my work.' She watched his face change.

His eyes brightened and she felt a kinship towards him for a passion shared. 'One day soon I would like to show you. I have great plans for my oncology research. Sick children can never have enough chances of cure. If it is my destiny I will be able to return to the world I love.'

Then he became a prince again and the light died. He pinned her with his gaze. 'So tell me how you think Fadia will take this?'

'Unimpressed.'

He smiled cynically at her. 'Succinct.' And paced some more.

Carmen sighed. 'She's brilliant with the boys but she is worried about how much control she will have over her life.'

He stopped and considered her words and tried to see what she was seeing. He remembered Fadia as a quiet but cheerful girl, watching him from afar, with shy smiles and even shyer laughter. There had been a time when they had been close.

Before he'd had to learn to be a man. Before his mother had left. 'She was always a happy little thing.' His cousin had suffered the same pain he had and he didn't want her to suffer more. He just wished he knew the right thing to do.

Carmen rubbed her forehead. 'This could really upset her.'

He knew that and he needed Carmen to watch over her more than ever. 'Then it is for you to be vigilant.'

He sighed and as if in slow motion his hand came up and he tucked a strand of thick black hair behind her ear. 'Between us we will see if we can return the smile Fadia's face. But for today my grandfather wishes to see his heirs. I will send ceremonial robes for them to be dressed in before lunch. The audience is at one o'clock.'

She'd bet that wouldn't be fun. 'Of course. I will see they are dressed.'

'I would like you to come.'

Carmen smiled and he felt the day improve with just one lift of her mouth. 'If you wish,' she said, tongue in cheek.

'As you appear to be compliant this morning, is there any chance you would wear the clothes in your room?'

She glanced down at her tailored slacks. 'Not appropriate for a royal audience?'

'I'm sure my grandfather would understand if necessary. Of course that is your choice. The palace seamstress was glad of the extra income. If you do not wish to accept clothing from me, you could always wear them while you are here and leave them behind when your tenure is complete. We would donate them to the needy. I will have her informed you do not wish the rest that I ordered.'

'So if I don't wear them I ruin a poor working woman's wage with my pride.' She looked at Zafar and he wasn't smiling so why did she think he was amused? 'Of course, if I may leave the clothes here, I'm happy to fit in with everyone else.'

He didn't look at her as he replied, 'You may even find our style of apparel is better suited to our climate than yours. Everything has a reason in Zandorro.'

Dryly. 'I'll remember that.'

'Tonight you are both expected to dine with the women, who are all anxious to meet you. They are very happy to dress well for the event.'

The women. The harem? Or the female relatives? Either way, she was the hired help. Oh, goody. 'And you?'

'I?'

She raised her brows. 'Who will you be dining with?'

He smiled as if he knew she wouldn't like it. 'Of course I will be dining with the men.' He inclined his head.

She kept her face bland and saw he was even more amused. 'After the meal tonight, I will bid goodnight to my nephews and I expect you to be there. There are things we need to discuss.'

And she was expected to wait around for that? 'Perhaps it could wait until tomorrow?'

'Tomorrow we will see the sights we discuss tonight.'

The King sat on a gilded throne at the end of a long hall. From the breadth of his shoulders Carmen gathered he must have once been a warrior like Zafar but his hands and wrists were twisted and thin with the passage of years beneath his flowing black robe.

To her surprise, his face, though lined, looked wise and compassionate. She hadn't expected that.

Two guards, surely Yusuf's twin brothers, stood on either side of him, wearing the curved swords she'd always thought Yusuf lacked.

Zafar headed their party. Fadia stood proud and tall beside him. Zafar carried Harrison and Fadia carried Bailey.

'Show me the heirs!'

The king gestured for them to approach and much of what followed Carmen didn't understand.

Zafar took Bailey from Fadia so that he held both. He stood tall and imposing, with a tiny baby in flowing gold robes in the crook of each arm. The twins blinked and gazed about as if searching for each other. Fadia watched her sons. Carmen watched Zafar. She saw the fleeting shadow of pain as he held the boys up.

Of course he would feel his own loss, his own investment in the future gone with his family, and she almost took a step forward to comfort him before she remembered where she was. That would not have gone over well.

Carmen closed her eyes. So much pain in this family. It seemed she didn't hold the franchise on that one.

After a few minutes of discussion with Zafar and Fadia in their native language the King waved his hand at the boys.

'Hmph.' The old man sighed. 'I congratulate you on your fine sons, granddaughter. They look healthy but must be renamed. In respect of your wishes and in honour of their father I name the future king Hariz, meaning strong, a ruler's name, and for the second born Ba Leegh, meaning eloquent and level thinking, to support his brother.'

He waved his hand at Zafar. 'They may go.' Zafar signalled to Carmen to approach and between them she and Fadia carried the boys from the throne room.

'I will see you later,' he murmured before he returned to the King's side.

So it was over, great-grandsons checked and accepted, and she and Fadia could just toddle off while the big boys talked. How her life had changed since she'd met these people.

So how much input had their mother had into her son's names? Perhaps Fadia did wield some power. An effort had been made to compromise. Hariz for Harrison and Ba Leegh for Bailey. She wondered whose idea that had been and hoped secretly it had been Zafar's.

She followed the royals back to their quarters. Every hour she realised more how insignificant she was here and became more determined not to be overwhelmed. Her sympathy lay even more strongly with Fadia. In a moment of trivial thought she wondered what Zafar's name meant. Probably big of chest or something.

She chuckled to herself and Yusuf turned and glanced at her. She smiled at him and he stared stonily back.

'Please to come this way. I will return for his Excellency this afternoon.'

They followed Yusuf obediently back to their wing of the palace. She couldn't help wondering what she'd do if Zafar went away. Apart from Fadia, she had no other allies in the palace.

Fadia fed the boys and they removed their robes then Carmen went for a walk to the palace garden to gather some fruit for her and Fadia's afternoon tea. The sticky almond cakes didn't hit the spot as much as a freshly picked orange did.

Soon it would be time to prepare for dinner with the women and then be ready for her audience with Zafar. She would do as she had been bidden on the small things—it was the large issues she wanted to win.

Like making sure Fadia was happy, and that she, Carmen, made it safely home when all this was over. With her debts paid and her heart intact.

That night after the meal, a learning experience she actually enjoyed with the women, Fadia stood nervously twisting her hands as they awaited Zafar, upset at the idea of seeing the man she was once betrothed to during tomorrow's excursion.

To Carmen's relief, when Zafar came to bid the boys goodnight he was quick to see his cousin's distress. She watched as he soothed her, his voice calm and gentle against her pain. 'You need a friend as well and he is a good man to keep others at bay. You can deal well together without pressure. I give you my promise I will protect you.'

Fadia nodded before she pulled away and looked with distress at them both. 'I'm sorry. I'm so emotional lately. My poor babies will think their mother is always crying.'

'It is early days. Less than a week. You have been through much. Be gentle with yourself.'

She turned and walked quickly from the room and Carmen moved to follow.

'Wait.' Zafar put his hand on her arm and motioned for Kiri to follow his cousin.

She sighed. 'I'm still so worried about her.'

He shifted until he could look into her face. 'As am I. But Yusuf will stand guard for the time being and Kiri will help with my nephews. Do you not need a moment to think of yourself?'

'I'm fine.'

He shook his head. Lifted his hand as if to move that strand of hair again but didn't complete the action.

'It will all be as it should. Trust me. One day she will be happy again. Tonight I will discuss with Taqu tomorrow's excursion. He is my friend and a good man, and knows we are keeping the King happy. I will ask him to come just for company. I must go away for a few days soon and you will both be alone until I return. At least ask her not to worry and try not to think about reading anything into his presence. Then we will talk again.'

Carmen nodded and Zafar went on quietly, 'Will you walk with me?'

'Now?' She tried not to guess his purpose but she could feel the nerves building as she waited.

'Why do you always say "Now?" when I ask you that?'

'Because you ask at the strangest times.' And I don't trust myself not to follow you into a deserted bedroom somewhere, she thought. She said, 'I'd hate to compromise myself.'

He smiled. ''Now is not the time. When it comes there would be no compromise.' No matter how hard she tried, there was no doubt about his meaning.

So there was to be a time? Did she have no say? She looked down at the sleeping babies and pretended to herself she was affronted by his assumption yet inside the temptress stirred and smirked. 'Their mother is still unsettled. I need to be here.'

'Kiri is here. As is her sister. They will watch over them. And Yusuf will stay so he can find us if we are needed. I wish to show you something. I won't have a chance tomorrow and after that I will be busy until I leave.'

So he really was going. 'Very well.' She dropped her pretence and glanced down at her palace clothes, worn for dining with the women, filmy swathes of fabric that made her aware of her own curves and left her with little armour to shield herself with against this man. 'I'll get my coat.'

He saw her glance and held out his hand. 'Your clothes are perfect. It is too warm for a coat.'

He took her through the palace, through a dozen different turns she would never remember until they came to a courtyard, the tinkling of the fountains the only sound as they stepped out into the moonlit night.

'Where are we?'

'At the south wall. The vehicles enter by the north gates and climb the hill.' He strode to a gate and selected a large brass key from a ring of many such keys. 'This is the other side of the palace and there is no descent to the desert from here.'

He gestured for her to precede him and they came out onto a walled ledge that hung over the cliff. The shimmering moon-bathed desert lay before them hundreds of feet below.

In front lay miles of undulating dunes, expanses of sand and rocky outcrops, all ghostly silver in the night so that she felt they were the only living beings as far as the eye could see. As if they themselves were on the moon.

She slowly turned her head and sighed. 'It's incredible.'

'When I can't get away, this is where I come. In the past it was the place I could find some peace, even if just for a short time.'

He lifted his arm and she followed the direction in the silvery light. 'Can you see that small hill under the moon to your right?'

It was surprisingly easy to distinguish. 'Yes.'

His voice lowered. 'There my family lies. I tell you not for your sympathy but because I am more at peace than I have been since the day I awoke. It began that day in the park, with new life unexpected yet beautiful, and you have helped me to heal.'

'Thank you for sharing this with me.'

'I know our ways are different, and I know you try hard to understand. But I want you to know that I see you. If it seems I am ignoring you, or have forgotten you, that is not true. I owe you much. When I am gone for a few days, you may like to come here and find peace for yourself.'

It was as if finally he was allowing her to see a tiny part of his mind. And his heart. She wondered how hard it had been for him and how much the darkness out here had helped.

She took his hand and laced her fingers through his, and when he bent his head she lifted her lips and kissed his cheek. She wanted to do more than that but it was time to go before she did something she regretted.

'Please take me back to Fadia.'

For a moment she thought he would protest but he didn't. Just nodded. 'As you wish.'

CHAPTER NINE

W<small>HEN</small> Carmen woke to the sound of Harry in the morning, it wasn't his usual royal demand. It was fear. A primal bellow that made her throw the covers and slip from the bed more swiftly than normal.

'What's wrong, little man?' She picked him up and glanced across at Bailey just as Fadia arrived. Harry's twin brother lay pale and still in the bed and Carmen's heart thudded with fear as she thrust Harry into his mother's arms, scooped little Bailey from his bed and tipped him over her arm to tap his back.

'Lights,' she called, and Fadia hurriedly switched them on. 'Get help. Tell them to get Zafar!'

Fadia ran from the room, her other son clutched to her chest, and Carmen laid Bailey down on top of the padded dresser and tilted his chin up a little to open his airway.

There was no chest movement but his pale skin felt warm as she searched swiftly for a pulse in his neck. Faint and slow, less than sixty, so obviously not her heart rate, she felt, but such a relief to have something.

She puffed three quick breaths over his mouth and nose and began to compress his little sternum with her first two fingers. One, two, three, breath, one two three, breath, all the while the pounding of her own heart threatening to drown out the world as her fear rose.

Zafar swung through the door, Yusuf and Kiri on his heels, and he moved in smoothly beside her and took over the cardiac massage.

Fadia arrived with Harry just as Bailey's little body twitched and he coughed and began to cry weakly. Carmen bit back her own tears as she stepped away, her hand covering her mouth as the restrained fear rose in her throat like bile.

She opened her arms for the distraught mother and hugged the shuddering Fadia as they stood clutching hands and watched Zafar. Yusuf handed Zafar a stethoscope and Carmen bit her shaking lip as she waited. Zafar bent and examined the little chest front and back and both sides.

Carmen chewed her lip as Bailey's cries grew louder and she hugged Fadia, her own need for comfort almost as great as hers.

Then she saw Zafar's face. Saw his cheeks suck in and his mouth work before sound came out. 'Good air entry now. Probably a choking episode.' He paused and blinked and inhaled. It was much harder to be calm now that it was over. 'We'll take him for an X-ray, though.' His eyes sought Carmen's. 'Tell me what you found.'

She ordered her thoughts in her head, strangely more focussed now she knew Zafar needed her control. 'Pale, blue face, not breathing. But skin warm and heart rate around sixty.'

'Too close.' Their glances met. Zafar shuddered, it was subtle but she saw it. She didn't think anyone else did but this had rocked him. Both of them knew how close it had been. 'Well done.' He took another deep breath. 'So fortunate you were here.'

Carmen looked up at him and he drew strength from her support. No doubt his own face was as white and strained as hers. His own eyes just as wide with shock. He knew later he had to hold her close, alone, so that he could banish the fear that would live, like the pain from the past, but for now he needed to reassure his cousin.

Carmen was saying something. 'Harry's cry was frantic. That's why I jumped up.'

'I, too.' Fadia sniffed and wiped her eyes and hugged her eldest son and kissed him before she handed him to Carmen, who hugged him into her chest with her own need for comfort. 'Harry saved him. I've never heard him cry like that.'

The two women looked at each other and Zafar placed Bailey gently in Fadia's arms and gripped his cousin's shoulder. 'It seems he is fine. Obviously your sons are designed to give us all grey hair.'

'Thank you, Zafar.' She turned to Carmen. 'And you, my dear Carmen.' She squeezed Carmen's hand in gratitude.

Carmen just nodded and stepped back further, bumping into Kiri, who was shaking like a leaf. The little maid slipped her hand into hers and Carmen, juggling Harry, hugged her to stop the shudders. She felt frozen on a treadmill of mental pictures. Couldn't help imagining if she'd been too late. If they'd been unable to save Bailey.

She squeezed Kiri's hand and turned away, and Zafar had no doubt she wanted to hide the tears he had seen spring to her beautiful eyes. They were so fortunate she had been here, had been so quick thinking, and he closed his eyes for a moment at the horror that could have been.

Zafar followed her and turned her gently to face him, saw the streaks of tears across her skin and the trembling of her mouth. He took Harry and handed him to Kiri and then drew Carmen in until she was against his chest. 'Let me hold you.'

Zafar searched her face, could see that shock had set in and needed to feel her against him and show her how much her quick thinking had saved them all. How bravely she tried to control the shudders that rolled through her body in the aftermath of horror. His brave Carmen. 'Thank you,' he whispered against her hair. 'Again. For caring for my cousin and my nephews.' He closed his eyes as the scent of her stirred memories of another time, of other comfort, and the strange way this woman felt so right in his arms. 'And for me.'

He spoke into her hair. 'We will take Bailey to the hospital and check his lungs more thoroughly. Would you like to come?'

Of course she would. She nodded under his mouth and he couldn't help the kiss he brushed against her hair.

'Then go. Dress. We wait for you and Fadia. We can bring Harrison.' He smiled. 'No doubt he too has concerns for his brother.'

The next hour proved reassuring as Bailey was X-rayed and examined again, this time by the head of Neonatal Intensive Care, and Carmen was surprised when Zafar suggested they leave Fadia and the doctor to talk while they minded Harry.

'Distressing episodes like this need discussion, and

she needs to ask everything she can. I think she will listen more if it is not I who tells her that all will be well.'

So Carmen walked around the children's cancer ward with Zafar, and tried not to think of those few moments in Zafar's arms. To feel him around her when death had been so close made her realise how precious life was. How easily lost. She shuddered as Harrison slept on Zafar's shoulder as they watched the children have their breakfast.

Inquisitive little faces peered at them from beds and highchairs. 'It's a lovely ward.'

'We tried to make it more like a pre-school than a hospital. And also so the mothers can sleep comfortably in their children's rooms.'

'And you designed this?'

'With the help of Dr Ting in Sydney. We had many discussions but it is a first for Zandorro and our staff are very dedicated.'

'And you gave this up when Fadia's father died?'

'It was my duty.'

She could tell he missed it. 'Perhaps one day you will be able to return.'

'Perhaps.' He slanted a glance at her. 'I'm hoping soon now. Another time, perhaps we could discuss the baby hotel concept and if it would work for sick children. If the whole family could come, and the sick child could visit the hospital instead of being admitted.'

'Of course. I'll look forward to that. For children on cancer treatment I think it would work well. I'm sure it would be less daunting for them without the separation of siblings.'

'Good.' He smiled down at her and she could see how passionate he was about this. 'We will discuss this again.' He looked up as a nurse approached and spoke to him. 'They are ready for us to return.

It seemed Bailey's all-clear had come through and she had an idea Zafar had been trying to distract her from the stress of the morning. Or perhaps distract himself. She couldn't rid herself of the idea he was still in shock and no doubt either of them would ever forget the image of that moment.

The ride back to the palace was quiet but there was a feeling of unity and support for each other that had previously been missing. Fadia kept her eyes glued to her sons and every now and then tears would well and then her glance would sweep between Zafar and Carmen and she would sigh and relax back in her seat.

Zafar and Carmen spoke quietly about the idea of building a child-friendly hotel next to the hospital for families and soon they were back at their rooms in the palace.

But always at the back of his mind Zafar could not lose the memory of Carmen's support in his moment of need, her quick thinking in Bailey's crisis, and as quickly as possible he finished the multitude of tasks he could not put off before he could return to check on them.

The female servants hovered around Fadia and her boys, and Carmen vibrated with a restlessness that was probably due to the stress of the morning, but it made his brows draw together as his glance lingered on her face.

'Would you like to walk with me?'

His heart warmed as he watched her struggle not to give away her relief at his request. She did need to lose the edginess that possessed her. 'I shouldn't leave Fadia.'

'Go.' Fadia waved her away. 'We are fine here and perhaps a walk will help you settle. You have stood and sat a dozen times these last few minutes.' She smiled at Carmen. 'No doubt your nerves are as bad as mine. The girls are here.'

Zafar nodded. 'Come. I will leave Yusuf here and he will phone me if we are needed. We will return in a while.' He smiled. 'Or maybe longer.'

Carmen followed him through the palace until they came to a part she hadn't seen before. The furnishings were more ornate, grander in the hallways, until finally they came to an entrance with a carved wooden door flanked by giant pots, then he stopped.

She knew. 'Your rooms?'

'We will have peace and privacy here.'

She nodded and he drew her through the doors and closed them behind his back. 'I need to hold you.'

She couldn't say no because her body still felt frozen in limbo and somehow she knew that Zafar could make her feel again. And she could help him. When she moved into his embrace he pulled her in against his chest and the strength of him made her close her eyes with the wash of comfort and relief.

'Thank you,' he whispered against her hair. 'Again. For saving Fadia, for saving me from another tragedy.'

She closed her eyes as his warm breath stirred memories that lingered of her times in this man's arms.

She sighed. 'It was such a shock.'

He shifted until he could look into her face. 'Yes. Yet you managed. But Yusuf will watch them all for the moment. I too need time to soak in the fact that all are safe. You need to let yourself be comforted for once.'

'And perhaps you do too.'

'I know you saw that. But for you we would just be at the beginning of more pain.'

'No. Anyone would have done the same.'

'Perhaps, but not as magnificently.'

He shook his head. Stroked her face. 'We were blessed the day Fadia met you.'

'Fate.'

'Perhaps. My brave Carmen, I just wish I knew what fate had planned for both of us.'

His hand rose and cupped her cheek then he leant down and kissed her. Firm lips tightly leashed with control yet full of dark emotion as he took her mouth and showed her he had been truly rocked by the morning's events. In return she couldn't help share her own horror and both grasped the lifeline, and a promise that they could forget how close they'd been to disaster.

For a moment sanity surfaced and she pulled back reluctantly. 'Can you let the pain go? Please. From now— and from the past?'

His eyes burned into hers. 'At this moment I need you held against my heart.' If only she could, and as if she'd spoken out loud he drew her back against him. 'The horror if you had not been there...'

'Let it go, Zafar.' She didn't want to think of horror in this moment. She saw his need. Answered it. 'You were there too. You made it happen.'

He tightened his grip. 'For once. Take the comfort I offer.'

But what if she lost herself? 'And will you take mine?'

That was all she wanted to do. Feel every glorious

inch of him against her; be crushed by his power and reborn with his possession. Stop fighting, for once, against the magnetism of this man who drew her like no other. Put away her fears of the ramifications she knew would follow.

His mouth came down and she sighed into him, let herself go, savoured the defeat of her fears, absorbed his pain and ached to heal it. Her shirt buttons fell away, as did his; she tasted his skin, dug her fingers into his corded muscles, soaked his strength into hers and gave freely and openly of her own. He lifted her and she wrapped her legs around him as she held his face against hers.

The world shifted under her as they turned as one, skin against skin, his eyes adoring as they skimmed her body. Then a shift, a shrugging off of more clothes, and she could do nothing but glory in his possession as she opened herself to him, her back against the wall, the rhythm of their need pounding in her heart until both were lost in the maelstrom. Soaring into the light. Suffused with heat like the desert that stretched away on the other side of the drapes.

Lost in a sandstorm of sensation she'd never imagined. Clinging to the centre of her world. Until slowly they returned to earth like the blown grains of sand outside.

They rested, panting against the wall, eyes wide and stunned at each other and the storm they had created between them, until Zafar carried her across and lay down with her still cradled in his arms.

When Zafar lifted his head the world had changed, along with his acceptance of the inevitable. He needed her. Loved her. Was endangered by her in his very soul, for how would he let her go? Staring into the shadows of his room with Carmen's cheek resting on his chest, Zafar inhaled the scent of her. He stroked the thick silken strands of her hair and a part of him died inside to think of her gone. What had he done?

A magical connection that had smashed into a million brightly jagged shards his foolish idea of perhaps loving her once and banishing her hold from his heart.

The most glorious foolishness of it all was he could not regret his heart's decision. He'd had no idea this was how it was meant to be. Or what price he would pay. All he knew was that if he did not return tomorrow, he could not regret this knowledge.

When they woke she shifted against him. 'I must go.'

Her forehead leant into him as his hand touched her cheek. She turned her head and with her own hand she stroked his fingers. With such tenderness she held his heart.

'Go to Fadia.' Yet even as he said it his hand tightened to keep her in his arms 'And later I will come to you.'

He sighed, captured her hand, and drew it to his mouth. 'We are going to regret this.'

'Perhaps.' So she realised that, too. 'But thank you.'

So he was already regretting it. Carmen understood because her mind had already accepted that this man was no ordinary man. Zafar the prince made her feel like a queen, more woman than in her whole year of marriage, more girl than a decade of flirtation, and, no matter what, she would always remember this time of mutual need as part of her destiny, even if their future could not lie together.

Later that night he did come to her but he didn't stay.

He pressed a key into her hand. 'I leave tomorrow. If I am detained…' he glanced away at the windows and then back at her, and she couldn't deny the flicker of unease his words caused '…perhaps unavoidably, then I would like you to remember there is magic in Zandorro as well as the things you don't understand.'

He sighed. 'I tell you that if I do not return shortly I have arranged for you to fly back to your own country as soon as possible. But in the meantime you may use the east courtyard as your private sanctuary.'

'I don't understand.'

'To have you here is a gift but difficult times lie ahead and I wish you back in the safety of your own country. As it stands now, there is no future for what we have.'

'Are you in danger?'

'I have safeguards arranged but I will be safer if I do not have to worry about you.' Unable to argue with that, she nodded reluctantly.

The next morning the sun was shining in through the windows when Kiri opened Carmen's blinds. 'Good morning, Miss Carmen.'

No. It wasn't. Zafir had gone. Probably into danger.

Carmen felt cold. Which was ridiculous. She was in the middle of a desert city. Eggs could fry on car bonnets. It seemed her heart lay packed on ice for its own protection.

She hated that here, as a woman, she had no power; she was not allowed to help Zafar. But, then, would Zafar even want her help? He'd hinted that they had no future. The uncertainty was stretching her heart to breaking point. She couldn't live like this. To be here was to be helpless.

She needed to believe that for her own safety. The safety of her heart. She was just a pawn like Fadia and the twins and even Zafar himself. As soon as Fadia was settled she would go home. The sooner she went home to the world she understood, the better.

Zafar was away for days and Carmen told herself she was glad. The distancing effect of time allowed her to see how powerless she was. How ridiculous her attraction to Zafar was in the royal scheme of things. How little future they had, no matter how she felt.

Thankfully every day Fadia seemed to recover a little more of her self-confidence and enjoyment of the simple pleasures in her life grew as she became more comfortable that Bailey would be fine in the long term.

Contrary to her fear, the older ladies in the palace were kind and helpful and doted on her babies and her. But the biggest change in Fadia was that from victim to advocate against Tom, against people who could so coldly plot the death of her husband, perhaps her babies. And Carmen began to see the fighting spirit of Zafar's family.

When the babies' feeding had settled into a routine and Fadia became more confident and her boys began to develop personalities that made them all laugh.

Hariz truly was the leader. Along with his demanding roar his little clenched fists waved impatiently when he wanted to be fed, while Ba Leegh would lie quietly, watching the world, observing, secure in the knowledge his needs would be met.

Carmen grew fonder of the young maid, Kiri, and her sister and the way they cared for Fadia and the twins.

And so the days passed but Carmen began to fret at being stuck in the castle. She never did get that tour.

Often she was superfluous in the boys' care now and took to spending an hour at the hidden eyrie Zafar had shown her as she prepared herself to return to her old life.

On the third day after Zafar left, word came to their wing that Prince Taqu, who had arrived in the palace the day Zafar had left, wished to take Fadia and Carmen for an outing to the souks.

'I do not want to go,' Fadia said as she wrung her hands and Carmen tried to calm her.

'Of course you don't have to go. We can say that.' Carmen peered out the window but she couldn't see the forecourt. 'Is that what you want?'

'Yes.'

'Aren't you a little curious?'

'No.'

'Fine.' She walked to the door. 'I'll go down to apologise and say you're too tired today.'

Fadia twisted her hands. 'Do you want to go, Carmen?'

'I'd like to get out, yes. But I can see the souks when Zafar comes back.'

'You could go.'

Carmen laughed. 'I'm sure the prince would love that. A strange foreign woman instead of you.'

'Let me think. Perhaps he could come back tomorrow and if Zafar is not back we could go out for a short time. I do not like leaving the babies.'

'Of course. But I won't promise anything in case you change your mind.'

Carmen's first sight of Prince Taqu reminded her

how much she missed Zafar. The man was tall, not as broad across the chest as Zafar, but a truly impressive specimen, and with a smile that promised kindness, not greed. She wished Fadia could see that she didn't need to be afraid of this man.

He came towards her. 'You must be Miss Carmen. Zafar has told me about you.'

'Prince Taqu. I bring apologies from Princess Fadia.'

He didn't look surprised. 'And they are?'

'That today she is tired. And her sons need her.'

'I am here for a few more days. Perhaps tomorrow.'

Carmen couldn't help her smile. It was too early to be sure that Fadia would but she liked this man. 'Perhaps. But the princess thanks you for your kind offer.'

'Does she?' Too polite to disagree with her. He shrugged. 'Or perhaps you do out of kindness. It does not matter. I will return this time tomorrow and ask again.' He glanced at his watch. 'Please tell Princess Fadia I await her pleasure. Assure her we will go out for a short time only and perhaps a change of scenery will assist in her recovery. And for your entertainment too, of course.'

'Of course. Thank you.'

On the fourth day, despite Fadia's misgivings, she and Carmen visited the souks, accompanied by Prince Taqu. Vendors bowed respectfully as they showed their wares, much less vociferous than Carmen had expected. No doubt their escort helped with that. Although the first day proved very formal, by the time the two-hour visit was over Fadia looked less strained and had agreed to another foray.

The next day, the fifth Zafar was away, saw them examine all the mosques in the city, along with a lei-

surely lunch at a city restaurant. Prince Taqu had studied at the same university as Zafar and his stories of
their escapades had Fadia giggling in a way Carmen
had never seen.

On the sixth day, the day Prince Taqu was to leave,
they went back to the souks to search for more trea-
sures for Carmen to take back to Australia. This time
the prince brought his daughter and afterwards they all
returned to the palace to show the young princess the
twins.

It proved to be a delightful day and by the end of it
Carmen's presence was barely necessary. Unobtrusively
she drifted further away from them.

She was glad to see Fadia more relaxed and there was
no doubt that Taqu had planned a concentrated assault
on the princess's defences. His promise to return the
following week seemed to be greeted with pleasure by
Fadia and already there was rapport between his daughter and Fadia.

Carmen realised her need to be in Zandorro was
drawing to a close, which was a good thing. Carmen just
wished watching them didn't make her feel so alone.

On the seventh day Zafar returned, and even the
sight of Yusuf coming towards her made her smile in
anticipation.

'Prince Zafar wishes to see you.'

'Where is he?'

'The library.'

Zafar waited. Pacing back and forth over the carpets.
Unseeing as he strode from side to side. Every morning and every night of the last six he'd looked forward
to this day. The day he would return to Carmen. But
now the day filled him with dread. Taqu had discov-

ered a spy in the palace and unearthed plans to kidnap Carmen and Fadia.

Imagine if he had not asked his friend to come and watch over the women while he had searched for the rebel stronghold. He needed to have Carmen safely back in her own country before the final coup attempt. If he'd realised how dangerous the situation would become so quickly, he would never have brought her here.

The door opened and she was there. Her face shining, her eyes alight, looking at him as he'd dreamed she would look at him. How had all this happened without his knowledge? To give his heart to a woman from the other side of the earth when his world balanced on the edge of danger.

To fall for a woman who did not understand the dangers. Who unwittingly exposed his own throat and hers. Who could prove his next failure to keep those he loved safe. A failure he could not bear to repeat. She was so fragile. So unprepared. So precious.

When she entered the library she didn't know what to expect but the distance between them came as a shock. Zafar nodded in greeting but there was no smile in his eyes, no move towards her, and she halted inside the door. Yusuf let himself out and closed the door.

'Is everything all right?'

'It is time for you to leave.'

CHAPTER TEN

THE words flew like darts from an unexpected ambush and punctured her euphoria. Destroyed her dream of him opening his arms to her. Mocked her anticipation until it fell in tatters around her slippered feet.

'Fadia's fine now and the boys are settled. It's time for you to return to Sydney.'

She heard the words, glanced around at the opulence of his office and unconsciously rubbed her arms. 'Today?' Go home. It would be soon but...leave them all right away? 'Why the hurry?'

Zafar's dark brows drew together as he looked past her shoulder. 'Your job is done. Your time here is over.'

Carmen looked away herself. To hide the shine of tears she could feel. She was such a fool. So she'd slept with him and that was that. And she'd been like a damsel in the tower, waiting for her prince to return. More fool her. Huge fool her. 'As you say, you want me gone. There is no reason for me to stay.' Still she wouldn't look at him. Couldn't.

She heard him move and her heart leapt. She turned her head and he was pacing, but not towards her.

Fool again. What did she think? That he hadn't really meant it and she could stay? That the royal family would greet her with open arms because she'd kissed him a few times? Slept with him once.

She lifted her chin. Well, damn him. That was that. And she felt remarkably, frozenly calm. It proved he wasn't to be trusted. She had reason to hate him now, which was so much safer than that other emotion. Why was that?

It all happened very fast after that. Her clothes were packed when she arrived back at the children's wing, Fadia was stunned and white-faced, Kiri sniffed and hid red eyes as she gathered all Carmen's things. In the background, waiting, Yusuf stood, arms crossed, impatient for her to say goodbye.

She was bundled down to the car, and when Yusuf opened the door he seemed surprised Zafar was already seated. 'I will accompany you to the airport.'

Yusuf stared at his master for a moment and then inclined his head before shutting the door. Carmen became more confused. The car started and within minutes they were leaving the palace behind. 'What is going on here?'

'I need you out of the country. For both our sakes.'

She thought about that and couldn't help a glimmer of foolish hope that he didn't really want her to go.

As he sat beside her in the limousine the darkened windows kept the interior dim and intimate. He didn't speak so she looked out the window as they drove through the winding streets. She never had got to explore on her own. She should have.

'I understand you saw the souks with Prince Taqu and Fadia?'

'Yes. I enjoyed it.' How could he carry on a normal conversation after the last half an hour?

She looked away again and a woman dressed in black with all but her eyes covered disappeared into a doorway as they drove through the big gates out into the desert. 'It's very difficult for a woman like me to understand your culture and customs.'

'But not impossible?'

'No. I should thank you that I had the chance to set out on an adventure to an exotic land in the company of exotic people.' Once started, she couldn't stop. 'Just as long as I remembered this was a job that would end…' she glanced away from him to the sand that stretched into the distance and her mouth hardened '…suddenly. But, of course, I am only the hired help.'

'Have you finished?'

She inclined her head mockingly. 'Of course, Excellency.'

He ran his hand through his hair and she smiled grimly. At least he wasn't immune to how he was treating her. 'Listen to me. You are at risk and I need to have you safe. I will not be responsible for harm befalling you.'

'I can look after myself.'

His eyes burned into hers. 'You will leave now and be safe.'

She narrowed her own, sifting through the mixed messages, reading between the lines. 'You said I could never be bowed.'

'Listen to me, Carmen. At this moment—'

A sentence he never had the chance to finish as gunshots rang out. Disjointed cracks like stones hitting the side of the car. She'd never heard them for real before but she'd watched enough movies to get the gist of what was happening.

Yusuf swerved the car onto a side road and suddenly they were airborne as they crashed through the scrub beside the road and into the desert along a barely discernable track.

The window between Yusuf and them wound down as Zafar pushed her onto the floor and he slid lower in seat with his phone out. His eyes held hers as he spoke rapidly into it and for some crazy reason she was too angry to be frightened.

'Three vehicles. They will catch us.' He nodded to Yusuf. 'Support is coming. They will meet us at the valley pass.' Then he turned back to her.

'I have arranged for us to be picked up in an armoured vehicle in fifteen minutes. We wait by the rocks in the crevice. We must quickly hide ourselves. It is too late to get you away. We must return to the palace until it is safe.' She shook her head. She didn't understand.

'If anything happens, and we get separated, keep quiet and unobtrusive and I will find you.'

'Why is this happening?'

'It is almost done but I feared this last assault. The last of the rebels have nothing left to lose. They wish to capture me but do not worry. Safeguards are in place.'

Now she was scared. 'I'm not letting you out of my sight.'

'Nor I you.' He grasped her arm and eased her up beside him. 'This is my world and when this is done it will be done.' He dropped a swift, hard kiss on her lips. 'Do as I command and you will be safe.'

For the moment the other vehicles were out of sight as they passed a large outcrop of rock and before she realised what was happening the car slowed. Zafar reached in front of her and pushed open the door on her side. She could see the sand rushing by.

'Go,' he said urgently, and pushed her so that she slid across the seat and out of the door onto the sand in an ungainly heap. He followed her and Yusuf in the car accelerated away from them in a spray of sand and dust, and suddenly the car was gone. She was in the middle of the desert, at midday, and Zafar was pulling her towards a crevice.

Zafar cursed his own stupidity as he crawled across the sand towards her. He'd known trouble was brewing but he'd thought they'd had another twenty-four hours before it escalated enough to pose a threat. And he'd dragged his woman into danger because he'd wanted to have her safe on a plane.

He froze. His woman.

It would be best when the fog that weakened him flew out from Dubai until all this was settled. His Carmen was a resourceful woman but the worry gnawed at him like a rat in the palace dungeons. All she had to do was lie low and wait to be picked up. Why did he worry she wouldn't?

The hurt he'd seen in her eyes would pursue him. She didn't trust him and he couldn't blame her. He had missed her like a limb for the last seven days until the communication they had captured had outlined the revolt. And the plan of kidnapping Carmen to force Zafar's hand had driven him back to the palace.

But the plan of shifting her to safety had backfired so now there was no time for thinking. Only surviving.

Carmen heard the growl of approaching vehicles and her heart thumped in her chest in time to the revs of the engines.

'Go.' Zafar's voice was urgent behind her. Spurred into action, she crawled inelegantly across to the outcrop and there was a crevice, sand crusted and pushed a couple of feet back into the rock, just as Zafar had said, which afforded some protection from the road. When she pulled herself in, it was deeper than she'd thought and she fell several feet down into a heaped pile of sand. It was dim, and something scuttled away from her hand as she tried to steady herself. Carmen shuddered and pulled her hands in close to her chest. Zafar fell in beside her.

The roar of the approaching vehicles seemed to vibrate through her body and she blocked out the animals or reptiles she'd disturbed to worry about later as she jammed her head down into his chest and squeezed her eyes shut as if she could squeeze the whole crazy ten minutes away. This was not happening.

That thought at least brought her some sanity. And Zafar's arms around her helped.

'Fear's your worst enemy.' His voice in her ear. She'd heard those words before, the woman on the headland, a test by solitary birth that Jenny had had to go through, and she'd said that to Jenny. Well, fear was in this dark and dismal hole right alongside them both, and she wasn't happy.

'Who are they?'

'Friends of Tom's.'

The cars roared past and the sound bombarded her more than the sand that flew into their crevice and coated their hair and cheeks. Her heart thumped in her ears, staccato thumps, and then she realised it was not her heart but the sound of a battle not too far away. An explosion. Then the whoosh of heavy fire and the rattle of machine guns. Then the distinctive sound of vehicles driving off.

Now beneath her own dread was her fear of what had happened. And even a little for the annoying Yusuf. Who was attacking them and why? And just how out of her depth was she?

Zafar stood and pulled himself up. 'Stay here. You are safe here.'

And then he was gone. The previous tenants scuttled against her hand and she shuddered. Zafar's footsteps faded.

She shifted onto her knees and peered over the ledge. He'd told her to wait there but she'd never been good with orders. The sound of fighting over the rise had been quiet for ten minutes now and she had a bad feeling about it.

The tenant brushed past her hand again and that decided her. She was out of there. If need be, she could come back to get out of the sun but she had to know that Zafar wasn't in danger.

It had been easier to fall into the crevice than climbing out, but with a skinned knee and three broken nails she finally crouched on the outside of the opening. She shuddered as she glanced back into the dark interior. It would take a fair incentive to get her back in there.

The hot breeze dried the perspiration on her face and she licked her lips. Sand grated against her tongue and she could smell the smoke that was rising from ahead. Thirst was an issue already but not one she could worry about just yet. Keeping low, she scurried to the next outcrop and stayed crouched as she listened. No sound from over the hill and no vehicles that she could hear.

When she made it to the top of the sandy ridge she

could see the remains of the battle. She gasped when she saw Zafar's car teetered on its side next to another burnt-out wreck of a Jeep. A collision with consequences, and then she saw Zafar edging towards the car. Yusuf!

She scanned constantly for movement as she skidded down the hill from outcrop to outcrop until she was ten yards from where Zafar crouched. He turned and looked at her; his eyes flared briefly then he sighed and shrugged. 'Of course you came.'

The low groan made her jump and she flattened herself against the rock and twisted her head from one piece of wreckage to another. It came again, guttural, weak and definitely masculine.

They crawled across the open ground to Zafar's car and peered through the smashed rear window. Yusuf. The man seemed trapped. Crumpled against the steering-wheel. The smell of fuel reeked. The burning Jeep smouldered too close for comfort. They slid around the chassis of the car until Zafar could stretch up and peer through the driver's window. 'Yusuf?'

With a struggle he opened his eyes. 'Leave here. It is too dangerous.' He closed his eyes and whispered, 'It is the will of Allah.'

Typical. She was getting so sick of men giving orders. 'Not until we get you out.'

Zafar was concentrating on the task ahead. 'Let us see if Allah wants you out first.'

He turned to Carmen. 'I cannot budge it alone. If we put weight on this side that teeters, maybe the whole car will fall back on its wheels.'

Away from the flaming wreck beside it. Neither mentioned that. 'Not easy to do that without getting closer to the flames.'

As they circled the car the tyres began to smoke as the building heat encouraged the fire to cross the distance between cars.

'We need a wedge, something to give leverage. We're running out of time.'

'Yusuf.' Zafar's command snapped the man awake. 'Reach the lever for the boot.'

'Leave, Excellency. Take the woman.'

'Not without you. Do it.'

She heard keys rattle and then the boot latch clicked. Zafar scooped out a large coil of rope and a tyre lever. And her suitcase, which she thought strangely thoughtful.

'We can do this.' He glanced around. 'That rock. Can you tie it there?'

She estimated the length of the rope and the nearest outcrop, and Zafar took his own end of the rope and tied it quickly around the doorframe next to Yusuf.

She ran and circled it until she had tied the car to the rock with as much tension as she could. She'd always been lousy with knots but the granny would have to do. The rear tyre burst into flames and smoke grew acrid in her throat until she coughed. They weren't going to make it.

She could feel the thunder of her pulse as the sweat ran down her face. They were going to be too late and Yusuf would burn. She'd really grown used to having him around.

'Fear is your worst enemy,' she muttered, and gritted her teeth as Zafar caught the rope and twisted it with the tyre lever to tighten it slowly. The rope creaked, the car creaked she watched him strain against it to shorten the rope. She ran back to him and heaved as well. Between them it finally shifted.

In the end it didn't need much, just enough to change the centre of gravity, and when it happened she wasn't prepared for it and the car swayed and then fell with a whoomph.

Yusuf cried out as he was bounced around like a cork in a bottle. Zafar wrenched open the door. A now unconscious Yusuf half fell out onto the road and she ran to help Zafar as the rear of the car filled with smoke. Flames began to lick along the interior roof lining as they dragged him free.

It was going to blow. She could hear the words in her head and she kept pulling, yanking, cursing this heavy lump of a man who had uselessly fainted on them, until he was partially sheltered behind a rock.

That was when she heard the sound of an approaching vehicle. The outcrop that almost protected them was too small to hide behind. Zafar pulled her behind him. Would this day never end?

The low throbbing rumble distracted them just as the vehicle erupted into a fire ball and she ducked her head into Zafar's back. A blast of heat singed the hands she held over her head and then it settled to a steady roar of heat.

The rumble became a throb from an armoured car, which slowed and then stopped beside their outcrop. Good guys, she hoped. Please let it be Zafar's back-up.

Two young men with machine guns jumped out of the armoured truck. One ran to the front of the vehicle and the other to the back as they guarded the road. A third climbed down and approached her with obvious relief. 'Excellency. Are you well?'

He turned a blackened face to Carmen and no doubt she looked just as much a disaster. He grinned and she realised he'd almost enjoyed himself. Men! 'It seems so.' He raised his singed eyebrows. 'Carmen?'

She nodded and after one searching look at her he stood up. Then he pulled her into his arms and kissed her. Thoroughly. 'I must go.'

Strange thing to say. She wasn't planning on staying either. 'Me, too.' A few minutes earlier for the cavalry would have been nice, she thought sourly as she peered through the smoke. Carmen sat up beside the unconscious Yusuf, bedraggled, singed and over it all.

'Miss O'Shannessy?'

'Yes.'

'His Excellency said we were to transport you to the airport.'

Now? Like this? A vehicle drove off. Of course he did. 'Yes. But what of your prince?'

'He has already left.' He reached down and helped her up. 'Our orders are clear. We have matters in hand and you must catch the flight.'

He gestured to the front soldier, who'd run in a crouching position towards the rise and after a brief surveillance had returned. 'His Excellency wishes you a safe journey.'

Carmen flew back to Australia first class from Dubai. After she'd been given fresh clothes. The strangeness of being greeted by name and with deference was both unexpected and uncomfortable. Yet all was overshadowed by the desolation she felt as the distance widened

between her and the man she should hate. Even the engines seemed quieter up here, which didn't help drown
out the ache in her heart.

On arrival Coogee was filled with memories of
Zafar, and everywhere she turned made her want to
run. And hide. She needed to get away. Maybe one day,
when it didn't hurt any more, she would return here.
She almost wished she could return to her double-shift
working life so she could fall exhausted into bed and
sleep, instead of gazing out the window and thinking
of Zandorro.

Instead, the next week dragged by as she tidied up
the loose ends of her life, paid the last of her husband's
debts, attended exit interviews, finalised the lease on
her flat, applied for and accepted a job in the new birth
centre in Yalara, the access town beside Ayers Rock in
Central Australia.

She had to go somewhere remote, unfamiliar, safe
from memories, for the next few months.

When some time had passed then she'd see where she
ended up. For the moment she told herself she needed
to meet her need for escape. She'd arranged for the few
sentimental possessions she had left to be stored in a
box at Tilly's and she spent the last night here before
she flew out.

Donna, the concierge, had arranged with Tilly a fare-
well morning tea at the baby hotel with a few friends
from both workplaces. It was the last thing Carmen
wanted but she smiled and nodded her way through the
morning until her head ached as she waited for the time
she could pick up her bags from her room and head for
the airport.

When she could finally escape towards her suite,

compliments of the management and ironically on the seventh floor, her head throbbed with memories of another time as the lift doors opened. At least the lift hadn't jammed.

Her room lay only a few doors down from so many memories and the corridor seemed strangely empty without a man standing guard outside the tiled entrance to the presidential suite.

Carmen's door lock clicked behind her and she crossed the room to drag open the heavy sliding door to let the stiff breeze from the ocean beat against her. The wind was up and she staggered a little as it whipped the curtain from beside her and flapped it against her head. The sting of salt lifted her face and she asked herself again why on earth she'd chosen the furthest place in Australia from any beach for her new job. But she knew why. She hated the weakness she hadn't realised she would be a party to. Her hands gripped the cold metal as if to soak in as much of the sea as she could before she left.

Zafar let out his breath. She was here. She hadn't left. He'd been to her flat, peered through the windows into the empty room until he'd driven to the hotel to hear she had resigned.

He'd managed to wrangle her room number from the staff, but not access. He'd also known she was checking out today.

He'd seen her downstairs, but talking to her there was impossible. How could he get privite time with her.

'If you take a room on the same floor, you're almost neighbors,' the receptionist had purred, giving way to his charm. 'And you can see each other on the balcony.'

It made sense. He'd known she couldn't leave without her baggage; couldn't leave without saying goodbye to the sea.

So here he was, and here she was.

'I'd prefer you to move back a little. I've had bad experiences with heights.'

She didn't turn her head but he knew she'd heard him. Felt her stillness. Prayed she would forgive him for taking so long to claim her. But he'd needed to finish it. Once they'd threatened Carmen he hadn't been able to rest until it was done. For the future, they would face it together, but for the past he had needed to finish alone.

Carmen felt his presence. Memories fluttered around her like butterflies in the sunlight. His eyes on hers, his wicked mouth curved and coming closer, his angled cheeks beneath her hand. She could see it all without turning her head. So he'd come back to haunt her.

She turned to see Zafar leaning uncomfortably around the privacy screen two rooms up. If he hated heights…'Then why are you out here?'

He moved back a little to safety now that he had her attention. 'I need to see you. You won't answer the phone in your room.'

'I haven't been in the room. What do you want, Zafar?'

One word. 'You.' One command.

'Still giving orders? Another quick romp?' She had to finish this. 'Go away.'

He crossed his arms. 'Not until I have had the chance to explain.'

Of course he wouldn't go away. 'No.'

'The flight was long.'

Tough. 'I'm sure there were other business affairs of state you need to do here.'

He'd had enough. 'Your room or mine?'

Impossible man. She needed to get this right. 'Give me a moment to think.' She turned and stared at him and his smile glinted.

'As you wish.'

See, that was the problem. She ducked into her room again. She had to bite back a smile. It had to be his room. Hers was so much smaller and he would be too close no matter where he stood. When the phone rang, still she hesitated. Was she agreeing to more disillusion or should she just get it over with? She let it ring again. But he would come if she didn't, she knew that, and she hated being a coward.

She picked it up, said, 'I'll come, but must leave for my flight in twenty minutes,' and put it down again.

It seemed strange to know he was there and no guard stood outside in the corridor. Zafar opened the door himself and stood back to allow her to enter.

She slipped past carefully and he didn't try to touch her.

She positioned herself in the middle of the lounge area, creating as much space as she could from anything that could hem her in. She saw by his face that he knew what she was doing.

The silence wasn't comfortable. 'Where's your staff?'

'I came on my own.' He smiled and the warmth in his eyes almost blinded her. 'Except for Yusuf, who is downstairs in the car. He does not dislike you any more.'

'Should you be here without protection? Are you safe?'

He shrugged. 'Yes, we are all safe. At last my country will have peace.' His eyes bored into hers. 'Alone is best for this goal I seek.'

She frowned. 'And what is your personal goal?'

He took a step closer. 'I believe you know.'

'No idea.' She crossed her arms protectively across her stomach and he stopped. 'But I do have a plane to catch.'

He spread his hands. 'Your flat was empty. Moved from. I was too late.'

'For what?' She was so distant. Yet incredibly beautiful. How could he have forgotten the way she twisted his chest until it hurt? He wanted to pull her into his arms and bury his face in her hair. Breathe her in. Tell her that his fears had overcome him, so afraid he could not save her. Yet she had been the one to risk all by his side so they could all be safe.

He smiled at her. 'I'm sorry I bundled you out of Zandorro.'

'You bundled me out of a speeding car.'

His chest shook with silent laughter at her indignation. 'Because I discovered a plan to use you against me. I thought you were not safe.'

'And would their plan have worked?'

He took a step closer. 'Because of that? Like a shot.'

'Don't talk about shooting.' She shuddered. 'Why are you here? It's a long way to come to say you're sorry.'

Just what was he asking? For her to make a bigger fool of herself? 'I need to leave here and decide on my future.'

'I have no quarrel with that.'

She blinked. Then he came closer until he was right beside her. Until his warmth seeped across the tiny gap of air between them. If she wasn't careful, he'd thaw her protection. 'I would like you to leave here and come back to my country. Then decide on your future.'

'I'm not going back to Zandorro.'

'You must. I wish to show you my desert.' He took her hand, and she tried very hard not to shake. 'Most especially the desert. We spoke once before about the desert but still we haven't slept there.'

The desert. 'I tasted the desert. When the sand flew into my mouth after...'

'Yes, I know. I threw you out of the car. Tsk tsk. So unforgiving. Where is that famous sense of humour?'

He was rubbing her neck. Smiling into her eyes, and the warmth was melting her heart. She stepped back.

'You're doing it again.'

'What?'

'Playing me.'

'Come play in the desert with me.'

'You come to the desert with me. I'm due in Central Australia this afternoon.' Sure now that he wouldn't.

She'd love to see his desert. Properly. With him. But she wasn't that much of a fool. 'Better yet. Don't.' She needed to get away. Just standing here talking to him was killing her.

'Is it too much to ask that I at least try to leave you with good memories of my country? Of me?'

She had to get away. Even if she had to lie. 'I have no wish to see the desert with you. I just want you to go.'

He stared at her, narrowed-eyed, and she remembered how he'd measured her when they'd first met. In the hotel. As if he was looking under her skin, into her brain. She tried not to fidget as she forced herself to hold his gaze.

Then he nodded. 'I see.' He glanced at the window and the brightness outside. 'Then at least let me drive you to the airport. I will place my jet at your disposal to fly you to your central Australia.'

'I have my own ticket. Thank you.' So he wasn't going to fight for her.

It was over. Her shoulders dropped. It was relief. Honest. She blinked away sudden dampness in her eyes and chewed on her lip. She wasn't sure why she'd thought he would stop her, and she certainly hadn't wanted him to. Had she? He'd only come to apologise.

'I insist. Change the ticket you have for another day. Cash it in. I don't care.'

'Thank you.' She wouldn't but he could think what he liked.

Zafar watched her. This was not what she wanted. This woman who had walked unaided from an ambush. Who had helped him save his man. Had he discovered his amazing Carmen's only fear—that he might not love her enough?

Ungrounded fear. He would give up his life for her.

He did not know why she had decided she wasn't going to give him time to woo her. Then, perhaps, she would have to do without the wooing. He wanted her. Badly. More desperately than he could remember wanting any woman. And he knew she wanted him. He prayed she did.

Ridiculous to be so obsessed with her, with the dream, Carmen with him always. The life he wanted, return to his real work, for the rest of his life. But life would be nothing without his Carmen. He needed her by his side.

'Or you could come back with me.'

'Why? So you can send me away again when you've satisfied yourself? Or when you decide it's too dangerous for me?'

'I would not send you away again. This time I will go where you go.' His fear had almost cost him that. She needed less protection than he'd anticipated. He would always protect her. His lips twitched, and he supposed if needed she could protect him. He did not like the thought but she was no fragile flower. His brave Carmen.

'I know it is different for you in Zandorro. As it was for me when I lived in Australia. There are good facets of all cultures and the world will be a better place when we learn to meld and bring the best out of both worlds.'

She looked back at him. 'Do you think that will ever happen?'

'Slowly, but surely.' He smiled and it wasn't fair. He melted her with those smiles. The chameleon. 'When people work together, miracles happen.'

The more he talked the more he wore the persona of the man who had attracted her so much here at Coogee beach.

The smiling god in the water.

The man after the storm with his head thrown back and his eyes filled with laughter.

Seeing him today had been worth it to leave her with these memories because those glimpses were lost in the prince. They were the dream man, not the reality. The reality had driven away from her in an armoured car. Sent her home. Gave her no choice.

'I did not have a voice,' she said. 'I can never live like that.'

'I know. I understand more than you can guess. I'm sorry you felt excluded. Forgive me?'

'No.'

He sighed but wasn't as downhearted as she'd thought he'd be. Typical. It was all probably a ruse to seduce her anyway.

'If that is your last word then I will drive you to the airport.'

She frowned. He was up to something.

CHAPTER ELEVEN

YUSUF held the car door open for her, and this time he bowed low to her. His face was still inscrutable but his body language was different. She touched his shoulder as she passed. 'Good to see you are well, Yusuf.'

'Madam.'

She slid in and Zafar slid in behind her. The leather smelt familiar, the tinted windows reminded her of another limousine, and how she'd thought Yusuf would die. How Zafar could have. Her pride was nothing to that fear.

He took her hand and kissed the inside of her wrist. Her skin remembered. It felt ridiculously right to feel her hand covered by his. She was hopeless. With his other he gestured to the space around them. 'Now we are alone.'

'Really? Must be a remote-controlled car.' She raised her brows and glanced at their driver.

'But that is Yusuf. He is with me always.'

'I noticed.'

He shrugged. 'I have decided to accompany you on your flight.'

She struggled to keep the shock from her face. Now

more than ever he mustn't know her thoughts. 'When did you decide that?'

'When I said I would accompany you to the airport.'

It had seemed too easy. 'Why am I not surprised? It seems my instincts to run from you are better than I believed.'

He was amused. Nice. 'Then why did you get in the car with me?'

Stoke up that anger. It was a good defence against the urge to put her head on his shoulder. 'What choice did I have?'

Now he was openly smiling. 'True. None.'

Too handsome. Too charismatic. Too close to her heart. 'So where are we going?'

He lifted his head and though he wasn't smiling she could sense his deep love of the destination. 'I had planned to propose to you in the desert but cannot force you to leave the country with me. So we go to your oasis. Your desert camp instead of mine. I believe they have luxury tents in the desert that watch over the ancient rock of yours. There I will woo you until you have agreed to be with me for ever.'

'As what?' She raised her brows. Fighting back the excitement as she drummed up some form of defence. 'Am I to be your concubine? Your midwife for nieces and nephews?' His bride? She was fighting a losing battle and she wasn't losing it with him but with herself. She loved him, had from the first, and she suspected she always would, even if she never saw him again.

She tried again. 'I have to work.'

He shook his head. 'Not for a few days yet. I wish to share the desert with you. At night. To show you the stars.'

She raised her brows. 'Is that all you want to show me?'

His strong hand stroked her wrist. 'What can you possibly mean?'

The conversation like foreplay. Like a teasing breathe on her cheek. Like the squeeze of his fingers against hers. 'Are you sure you're not going to try to seduce me again?'

He leaned closer. 'I certainly hope so. But you would still have the option of refusal. Or you will have agreed to be my bride.'

His bride?

The word hung. Loaded with meaning. Loaded with promise.

So belovedly arrogant. 'You have tickets on yourself.'

'Ah. Colloquialisms. We must teach our children.'

She laughed. Gave up. Leant across and kissed him, and he drew her into his arms. She was home. 'Let's not go to the desert here. I will see your desert first and another day I can show you mine.'

He leaned forward and pressed the button to lower the window between them and Yusuf.

'Stop the car.'

The limousine glided to a stop beside a children's playground. A little like the park where their unexpected baby was born all those weeks ago. Swings, a slippery slide, two little girls and their mother on a park bench.

The door opened and he stepped past Yusaf and held his hand in to her. 'Come. This is what I wish to show you.'

His hand closed over hers and she gave it and herself into his keeping. She had no idea what he was doing but she would follow this man anywhere. Anytime. And that was the measure of it.

He crossed the little park to the play pit. A small boxed area with white sand and a fogotten plastic spade. He drew her into the square and she glanced around, saw the bemused interest on the mother and the two little girls until she turned back to him and fogot everything else.

He went down on one knee. Her mouth opened to tell him to get up but she shut it again. The love that shone from his face, the way he held her gaze, the unwavering strength as his hand held hers ordered her to listen, ignore distraction, and hear his need.

'In this bed of sand, that symbolises my heartland in some tiny way, I, Zafar Aasim Al Zamid request your answer.'

He paused and the sun beat down up on her hair, his eyes smiled, though his mouth was firm and solemn, and she could feel the trickle of sand as it filled her shoes, and crazily, never had there been anywhere as romantic as this.

'Will you, Carmen O'Shannessy, be my soulmate, my lover and my wife, be by my side, bear my children, and love me until the day we close our eyes together for the last time?'

Her eyes stung and she blinked away anything that could spoil this moment. What miracle had brought them to this? Him to this? This arrogant, generous, tender, tyrannical, amazing man she'd been destined to meet.

'Of course.' It came out less definite than she intended.

He deserved more than that. And more strongly so

that it carried across the sand in a wave of truth like an arrow to his heart—like he had pierced hers. 'I will. Of course I will.'

She loved him. He knew it. Zafar watched her breathe in and moisten her lips.

'I love you, Zafar, have done for weeks now, and offer you all of my heart, all of my soul, and if we are blessed, my dearest wish is to hold your babies in my arms.'

His heart surged in his chest and he rose, brushing the sand from his knees. 'My love.' He needed her in his arms.

His lips met hers as they stood in a square box of sand and the giggle of children drifted in the breeze until they both pulled back with smiles.

'Come.' He grinned down at her with the giggles of children warm between them. 'Now let us begin our life together.' They strolled arm in arm back to the car where Yosuf held the door open.

'Return to the hotel.'

Zafar handed her in and slid in after her. The car started and she caught Yusaf's smile in the rear vision mirror.

CHAPTER TWELVE

THEY married quietly in the presidential suite of the baby hotel. Tilly and Marcus acted as witnesses and then they flew back to Zandorro with barely two hours to celebrate.

They stopped overnight for the formal part of the Zandorran wedding, a civil ceremony attended by dignitaries and the King, but finally Zaraf could carry his bride into the desert. It took an hour to reach the oasis in his helicopter.

Late afternoon saw them come upon a circle of tents on the sand beside a stand of tall palm trees, ridiculously like a movie set with shaded pool and tethered camels. An outsized tent sprawled in the centre of the oasis as large as a six-room house, and Carmen couldn't keep the smile from her face.

'You did tell me?

He frowned. 'When?'

'In Coogee.'

He smiled as he remembered. 'Before the birth in the park.' He nodded. 'That is when I fell in love with you.'

He stroked her cheek. 'Tonight I hoped we could share a traditional wedding night Bedouin style. Our official Zandorron wedding will take place in a month, when I can introduce you as a married woman. This night is just for us.'

A woman approached, vaguely familiar, bowed to Carmen and more deeply to Zafar. 'I am Kiri's mother. And Yusuf's wife. My allegiance is yours.'

Zafar smiled at Carmen's shock. 'See, others love you as I do.'

He took Carmen's hand, turned her wrist and kissed her as if the caress belonged only to them. 'We will meet again an hour before sunset. Sheba will help prepare your bath.'

Bath? She shivered. More delay. Rituals and traditions that she must now learn. Lessons for the future. She nodded, glad that she had spent some time with the Zandorran women and had an idea of what was ahead, but inside she held a little trepidation. She wasn't good at being pampered and by the smile in Zafar's eyes he knew it.

She gazed at her husband, a man she had already wed twice, and still he hadn't taken her to bed.

'Patience,' he said.

Patience would kill them both. But she had to smile. She loved him, would always do so, and she knew, without the shadow of a doubt, he would always love her. But after tonight they would live, wonderfully, she hoped prolifically, between their two countries, and his strong face framed that light in his eyes as he watched her go. Dark eyes that promised the wait would be worth it.

In the two hours that followed she discovered she could learn to cope with the hardship of luxury but the slowness of it would take some getting used to.

Kiri's mother, Sheba, took her robe and helped her

settle into a claw-footed bath strewn with rose petals and scented with oils that seemed to shimmer in the water. When she left there she was gently massaged with more aromatic oils and her toes and fingernails painted with colourless shimmer. Her ankles and wrists were traced with henna-coloured flowers and her hair dried and dressed in a coil on top of her head.

Then came the veils. Layer after layer, promise after promise to lie waiting for her husband to remove. Even the one that covered her face and left just her kohled eyes to stare back at herself, this stranger, this Eastern princess she had never planned to be but could never regret. Enough. She just wanted Zafar.

Memories of the caresses from their one time to-gether, the promise of a night in his arms with nowhere to rush off to. She could feel awareness gathering in her belly and finally it was time to go through to Zafar's rooms. The impatience grew until it consumed her and she tried to slow her steps, but too long she'd been a doer, used to being busy. This had all taken so long when she knew where she wanted to be.

Zafar's heart squeezed. Finally she was here! He'd been ready to tear down the tent to get to her. But the wait had been worth it.

The veils, her eyes, her shapely body. How he loved this woman. He could see her impatience, she made him smile. He too had been impatient and he would leave her in no doubt about that but seeing her like this...loving her like this, loving her as a midwife, loving her naked, loving her any wat she'd accept, as long as it was for-ever.

'You are so beautiful, my wife. Like a vision!'

The relief was there in Zafar's voice and she smiled at him. So he felt it too.

'Thank goodness you are, too.'

'My impatient wife.'

'My frustrating husband.'

He laughed out loud. 'Now I will introduce you to our traditional wedding feast.'

She rolled her eyes and he laughed again. 'Come, eat with me on cushions, drink from my cup and I will drink from yours. We will climb to the top of the dune and you will see the stars from the safety of my arms.'

Now that she had Zafar by her side, time passed swiftly. The wine they sipped tasted incredibly sweet, almonds and honey and no doubt secret ingredients she'd never discover, but its nectar left a trail of heat that coiled in her belly and spread back up over her breasts until time slowed to a second-by-second beat of the distant drum.

Tiny bells tinkled in the tent, discordant yet mesmerising music played softly in the background, and Zafar offered her morsels of flavoursome meat, tiny slivers of candied fruit and spoonfuls of rice so aromatic she closed her eyes. Each touch of his fingers to her mouth fired the flame that grew inside her.

When she returned the favour, he sipped from her fingertips, his eyes burning into hers, but his physical restraint was a more powerful aphrodisiac than if he had taken her finger into his mouth.

Never had she felt so aware of a man, so eager to feel his arms around her, so needing to be crushed against him, to be as one…

Zafar rose and held out his hand. His heart was bursting with wonder at this woman who had saved him from a darkness he had never thought would lift. Together they would achieve whatever goal was set before them.

'Come, wife. It is time we begin our life together.' She followed him to a platform of cushions set with candles, and outside a shadow guarded silently as they began a new dynasty that promised health and happiness to their kingdom.

* * * * *

Mills & Boon® Hardback

March 2012

ROMANCE

Roccanti's Marriage Revenge	Lynne Graham
The Devil and Miss Jones	Kate Walker
Sheikh Without a Heart	Sandra Marton
Savas's Wildcat	Anne McAllister
The Argentinian's Solace	Susan Stephens
A Wicked Persuasion	Catherine George
Girl on a Diamond Pedestal	Maisey Yates
The Theotokis Inheritance	Susanne James
The Good, the Bad and the Wild	Heidi Rice
The Ex Who Hired Her	Kate Hardy
A Bride for the Island Prince	Rebecca Winters
Pregnant with the Prince's Child	Raye Morgan
The Nanny and the Boss's Twins	Barbara McMahon
Once a Cowboy...	Patricia Thayer
Mr Right at the Wrong Time	Nikki Logan
When Chocolate Is Not Enough...	Nina Harrington
Sydney Harbour Hospital: Luca's Bad Girl	Amy Andrews
Falling for the Sheikh She Shouldn't	Fiona McArthur

HISTORICAL

Untamed Rogue, Scandalous Mistress	Bronwyn Scott
Honourable Doctor, Improper Arrangement	Mary Nichols
The Earl Plays With Fire	Isabelle Goddard
His Border Bride	Blythe Gifford

MEDICAL

Dr Cinderella's Midnight Fling	Kate Hardy
Brought Together by Baby	Margaret McDonagh
The Firebrand Who Unlocked His Heart	Anne Fraser
One Month to Become a Mum	Louisa George

Mills & Boon® Large Print

March 2012

ROMANCE

The Power of Vasilii	Penny Jordan
The Real Rio D'Aquila	Sandra Marton
A Shameful Consequence	Carol Marinelli
A Dangerous Infatuation	Chantelle Shaw
How a Cowboy Stole Her Heart	Donna Alward
Tall, Dark, Texas Ranger	Patricia Thayer
The Boy is Back in Town	Nina Harrington
Just An Ordinary Girl?	Jackie Braun

HISTORICAL

The Lady Gambles	Carole Mortimer
Lady Rosabella's Ruse	Ann Lethbridge
The Viscount's Scandalous Return	Anne Ashley
The Viking's Touch	Joanna Fulford

MEDICAL

Cort Mason – Dr Delectable	Carol Marinelli
Survival Guide to Dating Your Boss	Fiona McArthur
Return of the Maverick	Sue MacKay
It Started with a Pregnancy	Scarlet Wilson
Italian Doctor, No Strings Attached	Kate Hardy
Miracle Times Two	Josie Metcalfe

0212 GEN STD LP

Mills & Boon® Hardback
April 2012

ROMANCE

A Deal at the Altar	Lynne Graham
Return of the Moralis Wife	Jacqueline Baird
Gianni's Pride	Kim Lawrence
Undone by his Touch	Annie West
The Legend of de Marco	Abby Green
Stepping out of the Shadows	Robyn Donald
Deserving of his Diamonds?	Melanie Milburne
Girl Behind the Scandalous Reputation	Michelle Conder
Redemption of a Hollywood Starlet	Kimberly Lang
Cracking the Dating Code	Kelly Hunter
The Cattle King's Bride	Margaret Way
Inherited: Expectant Cinderella	Myrna Mackenzie
The Man Who Saw Her Beauty	Michelle Douglas
The Last Real Cowboy	Donna Alward
New York's Finest Rebel	Trish Wylie
The Fiancée Fiasco	Jackie Braun
Sydney Harbour Hospital: Tom's Redemption	Fiona Lowe
Summer With A French Surgeon	Margaret Barker

HISTORICAL

Dangerous Lord, Innocent Governess	Christine Merrill
Captured for the Captain's Pleasure	Ann Lethbridge
Brushed by Scandal	Gail Whitiker
Lord Libertine	Gail Ranstrom

MEDICAL

Georgie's Big Greek Wedding?	Emily Forbes
The Nurse's Not-So-Secret Scandal	Wendy S. Marcus
Dr Right All Along	Joanna Neil
Doctor on Her Doorstep	Annie Claydon

Mills & Boon® Large Print

April 2012

ROMANCE

HISTORICAL

MEDICAL

0312 GEN STD LP